I0622037

WELL-PLAYED

MESSY HEARTS #4

CHARITY PARKERSON

The scanning, uploading, and distributing of this book via the internet or via any other means without the permission of the copyright owner is illegal and punishable by law. Criminal copyright infringement, including infringement without monetary gain, is investigated by the FBI and is punishable by up to 5 years in federal prison and a fine of $250,000. Please purchase only authorized electronic editions, and do not participate in or encourage electronic piracy of copyrighted materials. Brief passages may be quoted for review purposes if credit is given to the copyright holder. Your support of the author's rights is appreciated. Any resemblances to person(s) living or dead, is completely coincidental. All items contained within this novel are products of the author's imagination.

—Warning: This book is intended for readers over the age of 18.

Copyright © 2020 Charity Parkerson
Editor: BZ Hercules & Consultants
ISBN: 978-1-946099-69-3
All rights reserved.

❀ Created with Vellum

INTRODUCTION

An ugly divorce left Bay bitter. Antonio has exactly what he needs. If Bay would let him in, that is.

After catching his husband in bed with another man, Bay is understandably a little gun shy. When he heads to Vegas for a conference, he never expects to meet a sexy Italian casino owner. Antonio has "player" written all over him. He's too much of everything. Bay doesn't want anything Antonio is selling, except he kind of does, and he hates himself for that weakness.

Antonio has.... issues. There are things he deals with that not everyone can understand. For that reason, he chooses his friends and bed partners very carefully. He watches people, reads them, and only plays with the ones who have that certain neediness in their eyes. Bay is the perfect fit. There's only one problem to Antonio's mind. Bay lives over three hundred miles away.

Distance and mistrust make the possibility of a real relationship seem impossible, but Antonio is determined to make Bay his. It's a good thing the casino owner is used to rigging games in his favor.

ONE

A CONFERENCE IN VEGAS HAD SEEMED LIKE such a great idea. A full weekend away that doubled as a tax write-off, and a chance to see his new friend Ford. Bay had been pretty excited about this weekend. As per usual for him, the weekend looked like a complete bust already. It was only Friday night. His first night here. Ford had already been to see him, only to tell Bay they would not be seeing each other again. While Bay hadn't expected Ford to greet him with a kiss, nor had he thought it likely Ford would rush to Bay's room with him, Bay had been so hopeful he had finally met someone nice. A few weeks ago, when Bay met Ford in Bay's hometown of Phoenix, they had kissed. A spark of life that had died on the day of his divorce had re-lit in his chest. Now Bay sat alone in the hotel bar. It was a state so familiar that Bay couldn't even work up the energy to feel sad. Mostly, he was just tired. Being alone was becoming more familiar than he had ever dreamed possible. He didn't think people were supposed to live like this. Yet Bay never seemed to live any other way.

"You sit by yourself a lot."

Bay's chin shot up as the heavily accented words washed over him. The same sexy Italian who had bought Bay a drink after Ford had abandoned him earlier in the night—to chase after another man, no less—stood over his table again. His gorgeous blue eyes flashed with something Bay didn't understand. He had the softest-looking brown hair with the perfect amount of curl. Bay didn't know how to respond. He was always alone. It seemed cruel for this gorgeous man to be the one to point it out.

The man who had introduced himself earlier as Antonio now claimed an empty chair at Bay's table. "I'll join you."

Bay bit back a smile. Antonio was obviously used to having his way. "You're awfully confident I want you to sit with me." Bay blinked at his own words. He never spoke to anyone with anything less than complete respect.

A low and wicked-sounding chuckle rumbled from Antonio. "I own this casino. It doesn't much matter if you'd like me to sit. It's my chair. I begin to see why you've been left alone, though."

Heat rushed to Bay's cheeks. He dropped his gaze to his glass. Maybe he deserved that jibe, but Bay's pride already stung from Ford's rejection. Antonio's words were lemon juice on his wounds.

Antonio leaned forward and set his elbows on the table. "You shouldn't look so injured by my claim. Most people are weak and can't handle a man as intimidating as you. I'm not the least bit weak. You don't scare me."

Bay was back to not knowing what to say or how to react. His mouth didn't seem to need his brain. "I'm not intimidating."

"Of course you are," Antonio shot back. "You smell like money and your shoulders are constantly squared like your confidence can't be shook. Men looking for a quick score will always find their gazes skimming past you, because you're not a weak target. They can't gaslight you and trick you into a one-night stand. You know your worth. A man would need to chase you, woo you. Treat you as you deserve. That's more work than most men are looking to invest. In this case, I love to lavish, languish… take my time. I am not your typical man looking to score."

The pure, unwavering confidence it took to say all those words at the same time was mind-blowing to Bay. "What are you hoping to achieve, then?"

"A late-night dinner date," Antonio said, as if it was the simplest request in the world. "I've been watching you tonight and you haven't eaten a thing. Let me take you to dinner."

Challenge rose inside Bay. Antonio was right on one point. He wasn't easy. "You haven't been watching close enough. I've already eaten."

Antonio's mouth lifted in one corner. Bay lost his breath at the wickedness in Antonio's eyes. "I guess we could skip the niceties, then, and go to bed."

Bay's eyebrows tried climbing to his hairline. "Wow. Considering I'm pretty recently divorced from a cheater, I have no desire to fall directly into bed with such an obvious player. I can see why you got into the casino business. If you don't mind, I have an early morning panel to attend." Bay stood, ready to leave. He fucking hated hook-up culture. Every man out there thought it was perfectly okay to fuck everyone they met. It was insulting, unhealthy, and disheartening. All Bay wanted was a nice guy and a quiet life. He didn't think he was being too demanding, but it didn't seem those things existed any longer.

Antonio jumped to his feet. "You misunderstand. Please don't run away before I can explain."

In spite of his better judgment, Bay stood still and held Antonio's stare. He didn't intend to believe a word the man said, but he would listen nonetheless. "Let's hear it."

A burly guy who looked like a human tank appeared at Antonio's side. "Nino, there's a man asking for the owner."

Antonio tore his gaze from Bay and focused on the new arrival. "You know that's not a request I usually honor."

The tank nodded. "I know, but you should this one."

A loud sigh poured from Antonio. "Very well. I'll be there shortly."

Bay tried sneaking away.

Antonio smoothly stepped into his path. "I'm a cuddler and that's all I meant."

The fact that Antonio had admitted that so openly and confidently in front of the one-man wrecking crew waiting for his attention was more than a little impressive to Bay. Still, Bay knew bullshit when he heard it. "This sounds a hell of a lot like you just want to put the tip in."

Antonio didn't bat an eyelash. "Give me a chance to prove you wrong." There was a certain steadiness to Antonio. Bay found himself relaxing, getting sucked in. Then Antonio pushed him over the edge. "Please?"

"I'm in room four thirty-three."

If Antonio had looked the tiniest bit triumphant, Bay might have taken it back. Instead, Antonio gave the smallest of head bobs while holding Bay's stare. "I'll be there within the hour."

Even though Bay wasn't sure he would let the man in when he came, he still returned the nod. As he stepped around Antonio, Bay couldn't help but drag Antonio's scent into his lungs. He smelled delicious. Bay's knees weakened. He stayed upright by force of will alone. No doubt Antonio would make Bay regret him. Bay was getting used to that. What did one more disappointment matter?

DERRECK HAD BEEN THE PIT BOSS AT LOMBARDI Casino since Antonio opened the doors over twenty years ago. They had grown together as men and had no secrets. Not that Antonio believed in shame. He looked Derreck's way. Derreck stood waiting. There wasn't an ounce of disapproval written on his face.

As always, Derreck knew exactly what he wanted. "Table eighteen. I'll find out about your new friend and get back to you before you head upstairs."

With a nod, Antonio headed to table eighteen, leaving Derreck behind to do the digging only he could pull off with aplomb. As Antonio neared the table Derreck had directed him to, his steps slowed. A groan rose in his throat. Antonio refused to let it fall, but fuck. A heads-up would have been nice. Antonio's ex Jett sat waiting for Antonio.

Antonio squared his shoulders. He felt his features harden. Jett's face lit at the sight of him. Antonio's voice came out harder than even he expected. "Jett. I told you not to come here anymore."

Sweet brown eyes batted up at him. He looked so goddamn innocent. The little bastard. "Hey, daddy."

There was no forgiveness in Antonio's heart. "You're no longer allowed to call me that."

Jett visibly pouted. He was so goddamned practiced at playing Antonio, but Antonio was done with being used by him.

"How much longer do you plan to punish me?"

Antonio drew a slow breath in through his nose. His need to please nearly crippled him. He couldn't back down this time. "This isn't punishment. We're over. Coming here, after I told you not to, won't change my mind. I have very few rules, but you've broken one that can't be unbroken. I do not share. It's time for you to go."

The chair across from Jett scooted away from the table with Jett pushing it with his foot. "Please sit, Nino. Just for a minute." While Jett had always known how to use his wiles against Antonio, Antonio was done. From the moment Jett confessed to sleeping with someone else, they had been over. There was no going back from there.

Antonio eyed the empty seat before turning a cold gaze Jett's way. "Consider this my final goodbye. You are not welcome here. Security won't let you inside again."

Without a backward glance, Antonio walked away. Jett was young and beautiful, but so were a lot of men. There had never been anything particularly special about Jett other than his willingness to do whatever Antonio asked of him. While Antonio knew it wasn't easy to find people who let him be himself, he was good at picking bed partners, and there was one man in room four thirty-three who looked like he might enjoy what Antonio had to offer. Antonio didn't have time for Jett any longer. He needed to find someone new.

Derreck materialized from nowhere. "Bay Vincent."

"Go on," Antonio said, deciding to let the matter of Jett being let inside the casino go if Derreck had the information Antonio sought.

"He's thirty-eight. While he currently lives in Phoenix, Arizona, he's originally from Virginia. He's a doctor. General practitioner. He's here for a conference on the latest breakthroughs in kidney care for patients with early stage kidney disease. He's due to check out on Sunday. That's the best I can do for now. If you want, I can probably have more for you in the morning."

A doctor. Damn. That was hot. Antonio fought hard against showing too much satisfaction. He didn't know yet if Bay would let him in tonight. Instead, he focused on what he could control right now. "You did good. Give yourself a bonus and I'll check back with you in the morning to see what else you've learned."

Calculating amber eyes focused on Antonio, pinning him in place. Derreck was always put together. It added an ounce of hardness to him that

Antonio admired. "What do you want me to do with Jett?"

Antonio spent a moment eyeing Derreck. He looked the same as always. Perfectly styled and with gorgeous dark skin, he did a great job of carrying off the professional part he played at the casino. The laugh lines around his eyes showed he wasn't always the hard-nosed man who kept the tables in line. There was something different about him now, though. Antonio couldn't put his finger on it. Maybe it was the way he said Jett's name. There was almost a loving caress to it. Antonio didn't think he imagined it. While Derreck didn't bat an eyelash under Antonio's inspection, he also didn't look comfortable. It seemed Jett had wormed his way beneath Derreck's tough shell.

A sigh escaped Antonio. He should have seen Jett for the troublemaker he was right away. Now he would have to deal with the consequences. "Feel free to do as you please with Jett. As long as he stays away from me, I couldn't care less what he does. If you want him, he's yours."

A deep line appeared between Derreck's dark eyebrows. Apparently, he didn't like getting called out on the obvious. "You're family, Nino."

Antonio waved away Derreck's denials before

they began. "Yes. I know. Don't start the whole blood of the covenant or whatever speech. I agree we are each other's chosen family, and nothing will change that. I never loved Jett and he is disloyal. Those two flaws together are one too many defects for me. If you think you can control him, enjoy yourself. Just don't forget he is more pretty face than good heart. Whatever you decide, I don't want to see him in this place again."

"Yes, sir."

Antonio fought the urge to rub his forehead at the response. It couldn't have been more obvious Derreck was irritated with him. Still, Antonio didn't try to stop him as he walked away. Derreck didn't understand. No one did. It wasn't that people were unimportant to Antonio. He simply hadn't found what he needed yet. Everyone he had dated who let him be himself only did so for what they could get from him. Antonio hadn't found the pure heart he searched for yet. Maybe it waited for him upstairs.

IN PAJAMA PANTS AND A PLAIN V-NECK T-SHIRT, Bay wore the carpet thin while he paced. He didn't know if he should have gotten ready for bed already or if he should have gone to bed and forgotten Antonio. All through his shower and nightly routine, Bay questioned his sanity. While it had—admittedly —been a long time since he had sex, he didn't think he was so desperate as to invite someone he didn't know to his room. Bay stopped pacing. Antonio's image filled his mind. There was something steadying about him. Bay couldn't put his finger on it. It was like the man's confidence calmed Bay.

A light knock landed on the door. Bay jumped like a bomb exploded. His heart raced into his throat. Bay sucked air on the way to the door, trying to slow his heartbeat before opening it. Antonio looked the same as he had earlier. Expensive suit. Perfect. Bay didn't invite him inside right away. He couldn't stop staring. Bay hadn't noticed earlier, because they weren't about to go to bed, but Antonio didn't have a single line marring his features. Either he never smiled or he was way too young for Bay.

"How old are you?"

A smile exploded across Antonio's face, disproving the first theory. "Forty-five."

"Liar." Bay didn't know why he couldn't stop accusing Antonio of being untruthful. He seemed too good to be true, which meant he probably was.

If Antonio was insulted, he didn't show it.

Instead, he pulled out his wallet and passed it Bay's way. "If I pass this test, is it okay if I move from standing in the hall?"

Bay stepped aside, letting Antonio inside as he flipped open the wallet. Antonio was indeed forty-five. In fact, he had just celebrated a birthday a week ago. "Happy belated birthday," Bay said, handing the wallet back. He closed the door, trying to focus on anything other than the man with curls he wanted to touch. Jesus. It wasn't right for one person to be so beautiful. By the time he turned, Antonio sat in the only chair. He had already taken off his jacket and was taking off his shoes. Discomfort always made Bay talk too much. "I'm sorry for calling you a liar."

Antonio glanced up. "No apology needed. It was a compliment. I'm rich and vain. Your accusation proves my money has been well spent on looking young."

Bay shifted from foot to foot. He didn't know how to respond to that. He chose to ramble. "I'm thirty-eight, which I totally look. Between always working and never sleeping, I probably look even older than that."

"You're sexy." It was such a matter-of-fact statement that Bay didn't thank him. Antonio didn't give him time to either. He stood and went to work, unbuttoning his shirt. "You're a doctor. I imagine you don't have a lot of free time."

At the observation, Bay's eyes jumped from where they had been savoring the skin Antonio bared to Antonio's face. "How did you know I'm a doctor?"

Antonio peeled off his shirt, making Bay's mouth go dry. "I own the building you're standing in."

That was fair. He was here for a convention for doctors and he had checked in under Dr. Bay Vincent. No doubt it had been easy for Antonio to learn that small detail. Bay was more than a little flattered that Antonio had obviously made a little effort to learn that much.

After taking off his belt and emptying his pockets, Antonio motioned toward the bed. "Get in. I'll turn off the lights."

For a half a second, Bay hesitated before moving to do as told. He had made it clear downstairs that he did not intend to have sex with Antonio. Bay wasn't set on that, though. Still, he would let Antonio try to prove he only intended to cuddle. This was a test, Bay told himself as he climbed onto the bed. An experiment. One of them would fail... or neither of them would.

Still, with the lights extinguished and Antonio

joining him beneath the covers, Bay couldn't help but try to push him. "Are you leaving your pants on?"

"Yes," Antonio said, sounding firm. "So are you."

Antonio urged Bay onto his side before he draped his arm over Bay and scooted close, spooning him. Bay immediately relaxed. He missed being married and taking turns being the big spoon. A small smile tugged at his lips before disappearing. He shouldn't miss his ex, but sometimes the loss still sucker-punched him. It wasn't Matty he yearned for, per se. Bay craved the companionship he had lost. He missed intimacy.

"That guy called you Nino earlier. Is that what your friends call you?"

"Only the people closest to me." Antonio's words brushed the shell of Bay's ear. Bay's body responded like Antonio had caressed his cock. He ground his back teeth, fighting the wave of lust that crashed over him. Antonio continued speaking, oblivious to Bay's plight. "If you'd like, you may call me that for now."

For now? Bay had no idea what that meant. A chuckle escaped him without thought. "Am I on a trial basis with it?"

"No. I think you'll choose a more intimate term for me, eventually."

"You're a strange one," Bay said, relaxing deeper into Antonio's hold. While there was still a tiny voice in the back of his mind, saying this whole thing was insane, Bay couldn't help but savor Antonio's heat. It was nice being held. Maybe Antonio would kill him in his sleep or was a serial robber. It wasn't like Bay had any real proof that Antonio owned this place. Hell, he could've paid some random guy to approach them and treat him like the owner. There were a million and one possibilities that were more likely than Bay having met a nice guy. With Antonio holding him, Bay wasn't so sure he cared if Antonio was a fake. That didn't stop Bay's tongue from wagging. "If you kill me in my sleep, make it look like you broke in. My mom would hate knowing I got killed inviting a stranger to my room." Even to his ears, Bay's voice sounded slurred.

A soft chuckle caressed his neck before warm lips followed suit. "You have nothing to fear, *Tesoro*. I mean you no harm."

"No one ever really means it, do they?" Bay was more asleep than awake. He wasn't sure if he had said the words aloud or only thought them. Bay should have been too uncomfortable to sleep, but it was like Antonio's touch was magic. Exhaustion won and darkness carried Bay away.

TWO

SUNLIGHT PIERCED BAY'S EYES, DRAGGING HIM from sleep. For a moment, he had no idea where he was or why his back hurt. When his memory returned, Bay groaned. He hated hotel mattresses. He had obviously forgotten to pull the blackout curtains closed before falling asleep, ruining his plans of sleeping late. Something else niggled at the back of Bay's mind. *Antonio.* Bay rolled over so fast, he made the back issue worse. He was alone. Disappointment tried setting in but was quickly dashed by the bouquet of deep red roses on his nightstand. Bay pressed his lips together, fighting a smile. There was a note tucked beneath the flowers. Bay beat back the growing happiness as he snagged the corner of the letter and dragged it to him.

Bay,

You snore.

Bay chuckled. How humiliating. He forced himself to keep reading despite his blushing.

Truly, it's adorable. It's only a soft, soothing snore —like a kitten.

For a moment, Bay covered his eyes. He was dying on the inside. This man. Where had he come from? Bay forced his eyes back to the page.

When you're ready, meet me downstairs in the restaurant. I'll buy you breakfast. — Nino

PS: you're a very sexy sight to wake up to.

Bay still couldn't believe how easily he had fallen asleep with a stranger. He was equally blown away by Antonio's respectfulness. As much as Bay hated to admit it, Antonio seemed genuine. Bay didn't know where to go with that one. Since Matty had thoroughly destroyed him, Bay had been on two dates. One with a guy named Jayden who had been understandably upset to learn Bay's divorce wasn't final at the time. Naturally, he hadn't seen Bay again. The next time, Bay had been more careful. He hadn't asked anyone out until he was officially free. Of course, it hadn't ended up mattering. His second date had been with Ford—the same guy who had abandoned him last night at the bar to go chasing after another man. While Bay didn't know the story behind that one, he knew it didn't say good things about him. Bay wasn't exactly killing it at picking guys. He wasn't sure he was meant to find love. Or maybe his problem was that he was looking for love when he should be searching for friendship. With a growl, Bay climbed from the bed. His gaze slid toward the roses. They were red. Red roses weren't friendship roses. Goddamn it. He was already dissecting the color of flowers. He really was a mess.

Bay got in the shower, hoping to stop any further stupidity. As he stood under the steady stream of water, Bay spaced out. The tiny details from last night creeped in. Antonio's smell. The way he held Bay. Bay swore he still felt the phantom brushing of lips across his neck. A ragged breath sounded loud in the small shower as it stuttered from his lips. His body stirred. Bay couldn't explain why such a small thing made him burn. It seemed it truly had been a ridiculously long time since he had sex. Bay ruthlessly turned the water to cold and finished his shower. He couldn't let Antonio under his skin. The man owned a casino in Vegas. Bay had a life in Phoenix. He was no man's good time. Bay didn't have flings. He wasn't that guy. Antonio had countless men filtering through this place. He could and probably did have anyone he pleased at any time he wanted. Bay was just another face. Just another body. He needed to remember that.

Bay took his time going through his morning routine. If Antonio was still there when Bay made it downstairs, they could have breakfast. Bay would even pay, but he wouldn't rush to see Antonio. That wasn't happening. Still, Bay somehow managed to get ready faster than usual. He always walked fast, because he had to get shit done every day. With that in mind, he forcibly paced himself as he bypassed the elevator for the stairs. By the time he neared the restaurant, Bay felt somewhat stupid. He imagined he looked like a small kid dragging their feet to avoid a chore. Then Antonio came into view. In a black dress shirt with the sleeves rolled up to his elbows, Antonio made Bay's mouth water. He looked relaxed as he read a book with a steaming cup sitting in front of him. He was gorgeous.

Antonio glanced up and spotted him. Even his eyes smiled as he set aside his book, openly waiting for Bay to make his way to the table. "Good morning." Antonio's smooth accent washed over Bay, making him tingle. Before Bay could choose a seat, Antonio stood and pulled out the one beside him.

There was no polite way to choose a different chair after that show of gentlemanly behavior. Bay sat.

Antonio reclaimed his seat. "How did you sleep?"

A smile tugged at the corners of Bay's mouth at the question. "Apparently, I snore, so I'm guessing I slept pretty good. What about you?"

The way Antonio's eyes swam with laughter made Bay's admission worthwhile. "I probably would've slept like the dead if not for trying to cling to every second of holding you."

Bay was at a loss with Antonio. There was no way this man ever slept alone, but he spoke as if one night with Bay meant everything. Bay didn't want to be anyone else's victim. Damned if he didn't feel like there was no way to avoid falling into Antonio's clutches.

Antonio cocked his head to one side and eyed Bay. "Why do you always look at me like you're trying to figure out which of my words are lies?"

Guilt washed over Bay. It wasn't Antonio's fault that Bay was this way. "I get that bitterness is very unattractive, but I guess that's me now." Bay's hands rose before falling back to his lap, showing he had nothing. "It hasn't been that long since I divorced a cheater. I guess I don't trust as easily as I once did." Bay's gaze slid away. He felt exposed.

Antonio took Bay's hand and held it between his. Bay's chin lifted. He couldn't look away from the loving way Antonio held him. Antonio stroked Bay's knuckles. "What an idiotic little child you must have married if he couldn't see what a treasure you are." He kissed Bay's fingertips, bringing Bay's gaze to his. Antonio's intense stare pinned Bay in place and stole his breath. "You don't have to fear me. It's okay to rest. I know you have no reason to believe me, but I'm not out to hurt you."

Bay wanted to believe. He was such a sucker. He couldn't tear his gaze away from Antonio's sexy blue eyes. He had to know. "What are you after?"

"I'm not sure yet." The honesty in Antonio's answer was like kryptonite to Bay. It was fine not to know. Not knowing meant he had gravitated toward Bay with no plan—like he had been incapable of stopping himself. That was more attractive than Bay wanted to admit.

Bay dropped his gaze to the book Antonio had been reading. Vulnerability made him uncomfortable. "Sci-Fi, huh? What's it about?"

"Anti-gravity," Antonio answered without skipping a beat. "It's impossible to put down."

A snort escaped Bay at not only Antonio's deadpan delivery of that ridiculous joke but at his serious expression. Bay shook his head. "Let me tell you, medical school will knock the joy of reading right out of you. This one time—"

Antonio shifted forward and kissed him. It was no more than a brushing of lips. Only enough to capture Bay's attention. The moment Bay fully turned his head Antonio's way, Antonio was there. His tongue swiped Bay's bottom lip. Bay automatically opened. Never in Bay's life had he been so immediately shaken by anyone. They were sitting in public. Bay forgot that part in an instant. Antonio's kiss was soft and loving—almost reverent. The way he gently held Bay's face between his hands had Bay fighting a sigh. When Antonio pulled away, Bay had to stop himself from chasing after him. His eyes opened and his breath caught. There was a flush riding high on Antonio's cheeks. His gaze was locked on Bay's lips—like he fought the urge to reclaim them. It had been so damn long since Bay felt this wanted. The power Antonio gave him was heady. Bay felt like he could take over the world.

"Let me feed you breakfast."

There was something deeper behind Antonio's request. Bay felt how his response mattered to

Antonio. He didn't know how he knew whatever he said now would shape where they went from here, but he did. "Okay."

The mixture of relief and satisfaction in Antonio's expression had Bay incapable of looking away. He wanted Antonio to always look the way he did now. Blissful.

"I'll pay," Bay said, hoping to make Antonio even happier. "As a thank you for my flowers."

Antonio's expression snapped closed. "No."

Bay blinked at the coldness in Antonio's voice. "I didn't mean to insult you."

Antonio's features softened. "Apologies. It's not you. I have no one to care for anymore and it makes me happy to please. I would very much like to be allowed to dote upon you while you're in town."

Oddly, Bay got it. He missed being a husband and having a spouse. There were so many small comforts that were gone now. "Being doted upon sounds amazing. I'm usually the one taking care of everyone else." Bay couldn't leave things at that, though. He was too awkward when it came to dating to simply let go. "But it's also important to me that you don't feel used, so I'll probably drive you crazy still offering to pay for anything we do. You can either ignore my offers or take me up on it. Either way, I won't be offended."

Antonio's eyes swam with laughter. "You're adorable. It's obvious you don't know how to let go and enjoy being spoiled, but you'll learn." He focused on someone behind Bay and snagged their attention. In an instant, coffee and orange juice appeared in front of Bay. Before Bay could finish doctoring his coffee, fruits, muffins, and omelets arrived. All Bay could do was watch Antonio's magic unfurl. "What's on your agenda for today with the conference?"

"I'm not sure. It depends a little on you, I guess." He fought a blush over the confession. Damn. Bay was so fucked up when it came to dating. He wanted to please Antonio, but he didn't want Antonio to think he was so important he would change his plans for the guy. An internal sigh rang through Bay's mind. It really was no wonder no one wanted to date him. He tried explaining in a way that didn't make him look like the mess he was. "I mean, I'm sure you have work to do around here. If so, I can find some way to entertain myself. If not, maybe we could do something. I've decided not to attend the rest of the conference. Truthfully, attending this was just an excuse to see a friend who lives in town."

Antonio rearranged Bay's plates so he could eat his eggs first. "There. Eggs get cold too fast to leave them for last. Is this the friend who ran out on you last night?"

"Yes." Bay refused to let Antonio's pointing out the obvious bother him. He had a single drink with his friend, Ford, before Ford's man showed up and made a jealous scene. No matter the reason, Ford had run out on him, and Bay hadn't heard from him again. That stung, but whatever.

If Antonio felt any way at all about Bay's friend abandoning him, it didn't show in his expression. "I don't do any hands-on work here any longer. The reason I'm always here is that I live here. In the penthouse. If you're no longer here for anyone else, then I would love for you to spend your time with me."

Bay held Antonio's stare, determined to be the confident man he was in every other aspect of his life outside of dating. "I would love that." After all, Bay recognized Antonio was a great catch. He knew this was a once-in-a-lifetime chance. Only a fool would pass up the opportunity to spend a weekend with Antonio, and Bay was no fool. He just needed to be an adult. Bay had to keep in mind this was only a weekend fling. He could do that. Surely he could.

Fuck his life. He probably couldn't, but Bay was determined to try. Bay would take this weekend as a small blessing and hold the memory to his chest to keep him warm. He already knew he wouldn't see Antonio again after this trip. Bay would find a way to be okay with that. He had to, because life was too empty otherwise.

BAY WAS PERFECT. HE VISIBLY FOUGHT TO BE brave for Antonio. Antonio grappled with the urge to stare like a crazy person. Hope was a heady thing. Antonio hadn't been this inspired in a long time. While Jett had always played his part, that was exactly what it had been—acting. Antonio craved the genuineness he saw in Bay. He wanted to be special.

Antonio watched Bay eat. The way he purposely kept his gaze averted screamed discomfort. He didn't like Antonio staring at him. It was a good thing Antonio preferred joining. "You're gorgeous. I imagine people tell you that all the time." Antonio swore Bay drew a little further inside himself at the compliment. He let it go. "What do you do for fun? Do you like to gamble?"

Bay's sexy blue eyes fixated on him, letting

Antonio know he was back on safe ground. "I don't bother gambling often, since I never win. When I have time off, I usually have so much stuff to catch up on that I don't get to do anything I want. I like to play golf," he added, as if just remembering he once had a hobby.

"I haven't played golf since my early twenties."

"What do you do for fun?" Bay asked, keeping the conversation moving.

Since Bay still held his stare, Antonio allowed him to steer the dialogue away from himself. Plus, Bay obviously liked talking about himself as much he liked compliments. Not at all. "I don't leave the hotel or casino very often, so I do enjoy reading quite a bit."

Bay's forehead furrowed. "If the place doesn't need you, why don't you leave?"

Truthfully, he couldn't avoid this conversation forever. Antonio had hoped they could put off the inevitable until Bay knew him a little better. Seeing nothing else for it, Antonio jumped in with both feet. "I suffer from severe anxiety. In new environments, I have panic attacks. So I don't go exploring often."

Bay set his fork aside and gave Antonio his full attention. Antonio braced himself for the psychoanalyzing that always followed anytime he confessed his shortcomings. A sweet smile touched Bay's lips. "I'm guessing, since you rarely leave, you must know all the best spots to enjoy inside. You should show me."

Goddamn. Antonio's breath left him. Maybe he would be the one swept off his feet. He refused to show how moved he was by Bay's offer. "You say you never win at gambling, huh? That'll change today. You should finish your breakfast."

Derreck appeared, anticipating Antonio's needs as usual. "I've cleared high-roller room three. You won't be bothered."

Antonio flashed Derreck a grateful smile. "Thank you, Derreck." He focused on Bay and motioned Derreck's way. "Bay, this is Derreck. He's the pit boss here. If you need anything, and I'm not around, he'll make sure you're taken care of."

Derreck focused on Bay with his best customer service smile in place. "It's nice to meet you, Bay. I'm always around and should be easy to find if you need anything at all."

"Thank you."

Antonio's gaze moved between the two men, observing every nuance of the exchange—calculating. He was learning Bay by studying his reactions to everything. Antonio wanted to know what made him tick. When Bay's sexy gaze moved back his way, Antonio's lips stretched into a smile that felt evil even to him. "Are you ready to win some money?"

Bay's chest expanded on a deep breath. His eyes flashed with laughter. "Let's do it."

Triumph brought Antonio to his feet. He couldn't wait to spend the day doing something other than drowning in his thoughts. Bay had no idea how he saved Antonio by simply spending time with him. Antonio would make sure he didn't regret it.

ANTONIO'S HANDS WERE ALWAYS THERE. GENTLY pressed against the small of Bay's back. Resting on Bay's knee. His fingertips traced the lines of Bay's palm. Bay couldn't focus on anything except those hands. It was such a small and crazy obsession to bloom, but Bay wanted Antonio's touch like he craved pizza. He fucking loved pizza. As Bay won another hundred dollars and Antonio's fingers linked through his, Bay broke.

He pinned Antonio in place with his stare. "How are you doing it?"

Antonio looked adorably perplexed. "What?"

"Rigging the games in my favor," Bay said, expounding on his question. "I never win and yet I can't lose today. How are you doing it?"

Laughter flashed in Antonio's eyes. "I'm good luck, *Cucciolo.*"

"What does that word mean?"

Antonio's eyebrows rose. "*Cucciolo?*"

Bay gave him a sharp nod.

Antonio's smile grew. "It means puppy. You're very sweet and adorable—like a puppy."

A snort escaped Bay. "I don't know whether to be insulted or embarrassed."

"Would you prefer I say, *Non vedo l'ora di sentire le tue mani su di me?*"

Bay blinked. "What was that?"

A wicked-looking smile shaped Antonio's lips. He moved close and touched his lips to Bay's ear. "I can't wait to feel your hands on me."

"Are you two ready for dinner?"

Even though Bay was lost in Antonio's words and his body burned with anticipation, he felt the way Antonio startled at Derreck's sudden appearance. He swore his own heart raced in sympathy.

Antonio focused on the new arrival. "I have too much on my plate already."

It took Bay a second for Antonio's words to register, and then another moment passed before he realized Antonio's upbeat response was actually a really, really bad dad joke. A startled chuckle burst from him before he could call it back. Antonio looked a bit mortified, as if he hadn't meant to say the words aloud. Derreck's closed expression never wavered, as if Antonio's bad joke was business as usual.

Bay couldn't stop himself. "Was that a dad joke? Do you have something you need to tell me?"

Antonio's blank features gave nothing away. "Sorry. It was a faux... pa."

Bay blinked. He was slow on the uptake and then a roar of laughter escaped him. He covered his mouth. It was such a dumb joke and it had taken his brain a second to catch on, but Antonio was adorable. He had a bad sense of humor, but still. Adorable.

Bay swiped at his eyes and slid from his stool. "Come on, gorgeous. Let's go find something to eat." He reached for Antonio's hand. "I'm supremely interested in what we were discussing before we were interrupted and want to hear more."

Antonio's relief was almost palpable. He linked

fingers with Bay. "I have plenty to say on the subject. Whenever you're ready, of course."

Bay didn't want to become enamored. It seemed wrong somehow to come to Vegas for one man and get swept away by another. The thing was—damn— he missed being touched. Bay missed the sensation of lips on his skin. He craved the delicious weight of a man between his thighs. He was lonely and he hated that weakness, but there it was. Bay needed what Antonio offered, even though Bay was likely not special to Antonio in any way. Antonio's company was special to Bay.

The minute they were seated at the same table where they had enjoyed breakfast and lunch together, Bay decided to speak his mind. "Thank you for spending this weekend with me. I know I haven't been completely willing to accept you at face value, so I appreciate your patience with me."

Antonio slowly nodded. "It's not personal. I know that." He leaned Bay's way and took Bay's hand between his. He looked so serious that Bay found himself leaning even closer. "May I stay with you again tonight? Just as last night, you'll be safe. I just don't get many opportunities to not be alone."

Bay's heart twisted in his chest. He wasn't an idiot. Bay knew this was likely a game. Antonio probably told a different man the same story every other day, but Bay didn't want to be alone either. "I'd love to keep you company until I have to leave tomorrow." He took a breath, hoping he didn't look like an idiot when things were said and done. "In fact, I'm hoping we can still talk after I get back home. And, maybe, it would be okay if I'm not completely safe from you tonight. A little." Bay couldn't meet Antonio's eyes as he spoke from his heart.

"What a beautiful temptation you are." Bay's gaze lifted at Antonio's claim. Wickedness flashed in Antonio's eyes, fascinating Bay. Antonio didn't stop drawing him in. "You make me wish I was the kind of man who would accept that delicious offer. Unfortunately, I'd never forgive myself if you left here thinking I only wanted one thing. In truth, I want everything."

A bottle of wine and two glasses appeared on the table, breaking the spell Antonio weaved with a sexy accent and pretty lies. "There's no way you just fell into my life with everything I've been searching for in a man." Bay shook his head. "It's just not possible," he muttered, completely forgetting the waiter's presence.

Antonio cocked his head to one side and eyed

Bay, as if he didn't know what to make of him. "Maybe I feel exactly the same way about you."

A light switch flipped in Bay's head. He thought about those earlier bad dad jokes and the obvious embarrassment Antonio suffered. Suddenly, the entire weekend looked completely different. He saw everything with new eyes. This wasn't some game. Antonio didn't mean him any harm. They were equally baffled by each other, wondering if this could become real. Bay sat back, feeling wowed by life. In the most unexpected of ways, and when he least envisioned it happening, this man fell into his lap. Bay didn't know what to think.

Bay shook his head, still trying to shake off the awe. "When I finally get past the shock of meeting you, you won't know what hit you."

A bright and crooked smile exploded across Antonio's face. "I don't know what's hit me now. That's why I'm adamant about taking things slow. I'm not sure I've ever been this blown away by anyone."

Bay's heart skipped a beat at the claim. "Then let me see if I can keep you interested even once I'm back home."

Antonio raised his glass. "Here's to new beginnings. I have faith."

As Bay clinked glasses with Antonio, he still wondered if he could seduce Antonio before he left town. He knew he should be over the moon that Antonio wasn't trying to get in his pants, but it was funny how much more he wanted Antonio because of that. Maybe that was Antonio's plan. If so, it worked beautifully.

No matter how hard Antonio fought against it, his hopes rose. When he had first spotted Bay sitting alone the day before, he could have never expected this much spark and intensity. The heated looks that kept passing between them through dinner made it impossible for him to walk Bay to his room. Instead, he claimed he needed to see to some things before meeting Bay at his room for bed. Antonio used his time alone to head upstairs to his penthouse to shower and breathe.

As he stepped off the elevator and onto Bay's floor, clean and ready for a night of cuddles, Derreck appeared in his path. His gaze slid down Antonio's body, confusing Antonio. "There's a hotel guest requesting a moment of your time," Derreck said, doing nothing to clear up why he looked at Antonio the way he did or why he had obviously been waiting for Antonio outside Bay's room.

Antonio decided to let it go. "There is absolutely nothing you can say to me right now that would make me go back upstairs, change back into a suit, and then go down to the casino to speak with a customer." Not only was Antonio wearing pajama pants at the moment, Bay was waiting. He was in for the night.

"They're claiming one of our croupiers cheated and are threatening to sue."

Antonio shrugged. "We're insured." He tried stepping around Derreck.

Derreck snagged his arm. His gaze latched on to Antonio with an intensity that Antonio had never seen before in Derreck. "Are you sure about this guy, Nino? You just met him, yet this is your second night in his room."

Antonio felt his forehead furrow. It was out of his control. "You've never worried about that before."

Derreck rearranged his features, going back to his usual judgment-free demeanor. "Sorry. I can't explain it. This feels different somehow and you know how I worry about you."

A smile tugged at Antonio's lips. He fought a

snort. "You of all people should know not to worry about me when it comes to men."

"Of course." Derreck's smile looked fake as hell. "Enjoy your night. I'll deal with our disruptive customer."

Antonio watched Derreck walk away with his heart in his throat. Sometimes, Antonio got the feeling there was something going on with Derreck that Derreck wouldn't talk about. Unfortunately, Antonio had never known how to get Derreck to talk. Antonio had always been good at reading people. It was one of the reasons he was so good at seducing them. Not Derreck, though. He never showed enough of himself for Antonio to know how best to help him when he got in one of his moods.

Since there was nothing Antonio could do about Derreck right this moment, he knocked on Bay's door instead. All thoughts of Derreck disappeared when the door swung wide. Bay was shirtless. He wore pajama pants and his feet were bare. Antonio didn't know where to look because he wanted to look everywhere before settling on Bay's naked toes.

"You know, I'm not really a foot guy—like no fetishes there or anything, but goddamn. Even your feet are sexy, and I'm turned on."

A gorgeous laugh escaped Bay as he stepped

back to let Antonio inside. Antonio tried not to look at Bay's chest as he passed. Whoa. He was just beautiful. There was a sexy smattering of hair covering some serious pecs. While Bay wasn't shredded like a gym rat, he was solid—like a man who could bench press a lot of weight. Antonio had to take a breath at the ideas that thought gave him. He looked like a sexy superhero.

"You look ready for bed tonight. I'm glad to see you don't plan to sleep in your work clothes again."

Antonio toed off his shoes. "I want to enjoy every second I have left with you."

"Good." Bay overcame him and worked Antonio's shirt upward. "Let me have this, then. At least let me feel your skin against mine."

Antonio obediently raised his arms and let Bay steal his shirt. He couldn't look away from Bay's eyes. Bay looked... sweet. "How are you single? You are too beautiful. Too... everything. Surely everyone must see the same things I do when they look at you."

Bay went still. While his expression remained blank, his eyes were intent—like he hung on Antonio's every word. "I don't think anyone sees me at all, but you."

"While I seriously doubt that's true, I can't help

but feel like everyone else's loss is my gain. You should get in bed so I can hold you."

"In a minute." That was all the warning Antonio got before Bay overcame him, claiming his mouth. "Damn. I've been wanting to do this all day," Bay said as he changed angles and came at Antonio from a new direction.

Antonio hadn't realized Bay had been walking him toward the bed until Antonio's back touched the mattress and Bay's body covered him. For a moment, their kiss turned heated, becoming the type of make-out session Antonio hadn't experienced in a while. His body was on fire. Bay moved against him like he couldn't be still—like he made love to Antonio in his clothes. Before Antonio could slow things down and properly seduce Bay, Bay rolled and tugged Antonio into his arms. Antonio fought to catch his breath as he pressed light kisses to Bay's chest. It felt good in Bay's arms. Warm. Like coming home. He wasn't ready to sleep. Sleep would bring the morning and Antonio still longed to hear every story of Bay's life. He picked the first topic that sprang to mind and ran.

"Will you tell me about your divorce?"

Bay groaned. It sounded unnaturally loud with Antonio sprawled across half of Bay's body and with his ear pressed to Bay's chest. Antonio stole the chance to rub Bay's stomach and sneak a few fingers beneath the waistband of his pajama pants while Bay was distracted by Antonio's intrusive question. Bay scratched the side of his nose, looking thoughtful before speaking. "Are you sure you want to hear about my past with someone else?"

Bay's question surprised him. "Of course. Your past shapes you. I want all of you."

After a subtle nod, Bay released a ragged-sounding breath. "Um, well, I suppose things started falling apart back when we moved to California. We moved so I could accept a position at a clinic for the underprivileged. Matty was excited at first. He's a massage therapist and expected it to be easy to get clients in our new town, especially one so close to Hollywood. I worked a lot. Too much. He started to resent me, rightfully so. The more we fought, the longer hours I worked. But, really, I wanted our marriage to work, so I signed up for a conference much like this one, hoping we could use the weekend away to reconnect. He was pissed that I planned to take him along on a working weekend rather than just taking a weekend to be with him. After we fought—again—he refused to go, and I went alone."

Antonio watched Bay's throat work, as if swallowing the bitterness before he started again.

"After one night alone, I realized I was wrong. I should've just taken the weekend off. Matty was my husband. He deserved more from me. So I went home the next morning. I stopped on the way home and picked up some flowers and wine. When I got there, he wasn't alone."

Antonio sucked in a hiss.

"Yeah," Bay said, dragging out the word. "Anyhow, turns out he was pretty relieved to be done with me." Bay cleared his throat. It sounded painful. "You said earlier that you don't have anyone to take care of anymore. What did you mean by that?"

That was a fair question. After all, Antonio had just demanded Bay's soul. "I have no living family and my last relationship was a complete disaster, so it's just me."

The way Bay eyed him left Antonio feeling exposed. "Do you see being in a relationship as you taking care of someone rather than making each other's life easier?"

It was the perfect opening, but Antonio wasn't sure he was ready to bare his soul the way Bay had done. Bay could walk away after tonight. He could run home to Phoenix and never look back. That knowledge left Antonio struggling with how to answer without showing too much of his heart. "My life is already easy. What it lacks is... a certain softness. I don't need or want help to pay for things. In fact, I don't need anyone for anything, except I want to be needed."

Bay cocked his head and stared at the ceiling for a moment before responding. "That sounds like a recipe for attracting a lot of men with daddy issues."

A surprised burst of laughter escaped Antonio. "You have no idea. It's like you've been reading my diary with that one." He swiped at his eyes. "I guess I haven't found that healthy balance of needy yet mentally stable."

A gorgeous smile lingered on Bay's lips. As Antonio looked on, the smile slipped away. "I'm needy." Despite Bay being exactly what Antonio searched for, he still wanted to argue. The sadness in Bay's voice made Antonio want to fix it. Bay's gaze fixated on Antonio. "Is needy the same as being in need? Because maybe 'in need' fits me better. I'm missing something vital in my life. Like you were saying earlier, I'm lacking softness. I don't think I was a good husband. In fact, in spite of Matty cheating, I think everything was my fault." He shook his head and boldly held Antonio's stare. "I know it was my fault. He tried in a thousand ways to tell me I was failing him. That he was lonely and unhappy. He tried to always make our house a home and I soaked up everything he gave while giving nothing back. It's too late to go back, and we've both moved on, but I miss the softness." A bitter smile touched Bay's lips. "Nowadays, the world is different. It's dating apps and one-night stands. The world is a prescription for heartbreak, and I don't think I have another loss left in me to give to anyone else. So I don't try." His gaze moved over Antonio's face, as if searching for something only he could see. "I want to believe you're real, but—honestly—you seem too good to be true. In my experience, even the men you think you can trust can't be trusted. It seems pretty hopeless there's any chance you'll be different."

Antonio couldn't fight his smile. Bay had no idea what he was in for with Antonio. "One of these days, you'll think about this moment, and you'll wonder why you couldn't see the real me."

A sexy rumble of laughter fell from Bay's lips. "I have no idea what that means."

He wouldn't explain. Bay would understand soon enough. "May I kiss you again?"

Bay's heart was in his eyes. "You don't have to ask."

A smile that felt wicked even to him stretched Antonio's lips. "But it felt nice to be asked, didn't it?"

Instead of answering, Bay rolled and pinned Antonio beneath him. A half second before their lips met, Bay whispered, "It felt amazing."

Antonio swore even his heart smiled as their tongues brushed. Life hadn't left Bay untouched, but he didn't know Antonio. Some guy had been fucking someone else and still managed to make Bay believe that it was his fault he had been cheated on. Fuck that. Antonio could show him a different life. He planned to sweep Bay off his feet. Bay hadn't known romance before now. Antonio might suffer from crippling anxiety that forced him to seek validation from men, but he also knew exactly how to get the affirmation he needed—by being very, very good at seduction. Bay didn't stand a chance.

THREE

THE DAY HAD BEEN LONG, SEEING PATIENTS AND catching up. Bay swung wildly between mentally sighing every time he thought about Antonio and silently panicking that he would never see the man again. He spent the first half of his day setting up a surprise for Antonio. The second half of his day Bay spent worrying he looked desperate. Antonio made him a mess. Bay hadn't decided if that was a good or bad thing yet.

"How did the symposium go?"

Bay looked up from his laptop and focused on Teagan, the nurse practitioner who had been working with him since Bay moved to Phoenix a year ago to be closer to his grandmother before she passed. Also, to get away from Matty, but that was a different topic.

"It was good." Damn, it was amazing. Bay fought the urge to go back to Vegas right that second.

"Did you learn anything we can apply to patients immediately?"

Bay blinked at the question. "What?"

Teagan laughed. Her eyes swam with inner happiness. "Kidney disease. The conference. Did you learn anything?"

Heat rose in Bay's cheeks. "Yeah, no. Sorry. It was pretty general knowledge stuff. I didn't hear anything I hadn't heard before." Especially since he had only gone to one panel.

"Plus, it was Vegas," she said knowingly. Teagan moved farther into the room. "Seriously, why won't you take a real vacation? Everyone needs some time off. You have like four weeks built up you could be taking, but you don't."

She hadn't said anything Bay didn't know or that he hadn't been thinking seriously about. "Yeah. This past weekend made me realize how much I'm missing. As a matter of fact, I was just going over my schedule, trying to decide how disruptive it would be to the clinic if I took a trip."

"Wow." Teagan sat in the empty chair across from Bay. "What's his name?"

Bay fought to keep his expression neutral. "I don't know what you mean." He immediately broke. "Antonio. He's Italian."

"Oooh. Tell me more."

A smile that felt huge and idiotic even to Bay stretched his lips. "Dark hair, blue eyes, and looks twenty years younger than me, even though he isn't. Very sexy. He owns a casino."

"Jesus," Teagan breathed, sounding intrigued. "How did you come back here? I think I would've settled in and let a sugar daddy have his way."

Bay laughed. He had always liked Teagan. She was funny and didn't care much about roles. Teagan was pretty unapologetically herself all the time. Bay appreciated that honesty in a fake world.

"I got the impression he's a little tired of always being seen as the sugar daddy."

A knowing smile stretched Teagan's lips. She tossed the long braid that had fallen over her shoulder behind her. "Well, then. You have to stand out and spoil him instead. I imagine that's not something he's seen."

Bay nodded. "That's my plan, but—truthfully—

we live in different states and both have ties to where we currently live. I'll admit I'm beginning to wonder if I should pursue this. Maybe I'm wasting both our time."

Teagan made a rude noise and curled her nose. "Screw all that noise. Life doesn't have to be about looking for a soul mate. Sometimes, it's just about meeting someone new. My advice is to just have fun with this. Lose some dignity on Skype and grab some happiness. Even if the relationship doesn't last a lifetime, the memories will."

Bay took a deep breath and let Teagan's words sink in. Maybe she was right. He didn't need to think so much about whether this was going anywhere. Maybe he would just grab some happiness. Bay needed a little of that. He thought—possibly—Antonio did too. Bay had exactly what he needed. He would start working on making Antonio smile today and let tomorrow sort itself out. Bay could do that... Maybe.

LIFE HAD BEEN A LITTLE TOO QUIET SINCE BAY left. Antonio's world was already small and lonely.

He only met people if they came through the casino or if they came to him after meeting online. That made life harder than anyone realized. It wasn't that he couldn't go places. He had money. Antonio could board a private plane and go anywhere with minimal discomfort. He could hire a car to take him to a secluded place where he enjoyed a new location alone. It wasn't like he never left the casino. He went places. The doctor. The store. Sometimes, he even went through drive-thrus. His life wasn't empty. Yet it still felt like it today.

Antonio headed for the elevator. He would go to bed. Alone. There was no time like the present to get ready to do all the same shit by himself tomorrow. He knew he was being maudlin. Antonio couldn't help it. Sometimes, being this way got to him. For all his willingness to do new things in business, he wasn't strong socially. He was too old to think that would change. The chances he would get up and decide to go clubbing tomorrow night were very thin.

Derreck stepped into his path, smiling like an idiot. "I just took a package up to your penthouse."

"Okay." Derreck's good humor confused him. It was a package. Antonio got those all the time.

"It's a present from your sexy doctor. You must've made quite an impression."

Happiness surged through him. Antonio had to force himself to stay put. He wanted to race upstairs. "Thank you for letting me know. I'm headed that way now."

Derreck snorted, obviously seeing Antonio's game for what it was. "Okay. I see. You're playing this one close to your chest. I don't get any details at all."

Antonio smiled at Derreck's antics, even though Derreck wasn't completely wrong. Antonio wasn't quite ready to share his thoughts on Bay yet. There was something a little different about him than the men Antonio usually chose. "It's too early for gossip. Sending presents is a good sign, but I'm not sure I've won him yet."

Derreck snorted again. "Well, I am," Derreck said with a chuckle as he walked away. "Have a good night, Nino," he added over his shoulder as he passed.

"You too," Antonio muttered under his breath with his mind locked on Derreck's reaction. He wondered what Derreck saw that he didn't. The question had Antonio hurrying upstairs.

As he stepped off the elevator onto his private floor, there was no missing his package. A large box sat in the center of Antonio's living room. He eyed it as he moved closer. Even with Derreck's warning, Antonio was taken aback. Antonio had been expecting flowers or something similar based on Derreck's smile and knowing expression. This was something else altogether. The box was big enough for Bay to have shipped himself. Even though he knew that wasn't the case, the thought still had him crossing the room. There was a card on top. He peeled opened the tab on the envelope and pulled out the card. It had a fluffy-looking dog on the front. Antonio flipped it open. Only a handwritten note was inside.

Nino,

Open your gift and then come back to read me.

With a snort, Antonio set the card aside, dug out his pocket knife, and cut open the box. There were a few items inside. First, a pillow that was a gigantic U. It was easily six feet on the two long sides and three feet in the center. Next was a weighted blanket. Underneath everything was a brightly colored stuffed unicorn. Antonio repacked the box and went back to the card.

Take everything to bed and then read me.

A rumble of laughter gathered in Antonio's throat. He collected everything, including the card, and dragged it to the bed. After removing everything from their respective packages, he piled his presents on the bed. With that done, Antonio decided he might as well be comfortable. He changed into pajama pants, leaving off his shirt, and then climbed into bed. As he settled into the pillow cocoon, he pulled the weighted blanket over him, tucking the unicorn in with him before snagging the card again.

If you're all settled in, call me. I miss you.

The smile stretching his lips was out of his control as Antonio immediately hit the FaceTime icon on his phone. It wasn't enough to hear Bay's voice; he needed to see him.

Bay's face appeared on the phone. His hair stood in every direction and there were dark circles under his eyes, making him look exhausted. Despite those things, he looked fucking gorgeous. His smile had Antonio wishing he could kiss him. "Hey, gorgeous. I see you got my presents."

Antonio moved the unicorn's face into camera view. "Yes. Thank you. Sparkle Feet and I are snuggling and missing you."

Bay's eyes danced with laughter. "Sparkle Feet?"

Happiness grew larger inside Antonio by the second. He nodded. "Sure. He has sparkly feet and needed a name." Bay smothered a yawn and Antonio's smile slipped away. "Are you okay?"

A sweet smile passed over Bay's features. "Yeah. Sorry. It's been a long day. I think two days off in a row reminded my body what it's like to rest. Now it's protesting the abuse."

"Do you not get vacation time?"

Bay nodded as he shifted positions. He leaned the phone against something before settling his head on his arm and focusing on Antonio. It looked like he was at a desk. "Yeah. I guess I should think about using it sometime."

"Are you still at work?"

A sexy rumble of laughter caressed Antonio's ears. "Maybe."

Confusion had Antonio's forehead furrowing. "Why?"

"Honestly? There's nothing at my place but a bunch of empty rooms. I may as well make myself useful elsewhere."

"What if you had a reason to come home?" The question was out of impulse. Antonio didn't take it back.

"Then I would go home."

Antonio needed a minute to think. He changed the subject to buy himself some time. "This is an odd assortment of gifts you sent. I love everything. It's just unique."

"It's specific to you," Bay said, as if surprised Antonio couldn't see the obvious. "You like to cuddle, but I had to come home. The pillow is meant to simulate being held, so is the weighted blanket. Sparkle Feet is an bonus. He gives you something to hold on to no matter how much you toss and turn." A heart-melting smile touched Bay's lips. "Until we're together again, that is."

Antonio's impulses were back to being out of control. "What if I came to you?"

Bay's smile slipped away. "I thought you didn't leave your casino."

"I do. Just not often. I mean, I could book a private flight and come to you. If you'd like..." Antonio left the offer hanging there, ready to snatch it back if Bay didn't seem interested.

Bay's lips slowly curved into a smile. "Really?" He looked just like an excited child. His eyes practically glowed with happiness. "You could stay with me, if you want. Then I could come home to you every night. In fact, I could probably take some time off so you're not stuck alone in the house."

Antonio shrugged. "It's whatever you want. I'd love for you to take some time off, so you can rest, but you don't have to do it for me. I'm pretty good at entertaining myself."

"How long could you stay?" Bay asked, avoiding Antonio's claim.

"However long you'd like, I suppose. This place pretty much runs without me. I could just come and then we could figure it out. If you get sick of me after a few days, I'll come home."

Bay bit his lip. It did nothing to hide his happiness. "I would love that. It's odd, I know, because we just met, but I really like you, Nino."

The ugly possessiveness that always had Antonio destroying people rose in his chest. He wanted Bay. "I like you too. Probably a lot more than I should. So, am I coming?"

A bright smile exploded across Bay's face. "Yes. You definitely are."

The double entendre in Bay's words couldn't be missed. "Listen to you. So positive I'm a sure thing."

Bay's face reddened. "I didn't mean—"

"I am, of course," Antonio said, cutting Bay off before he backed out of anything. "Sparkle Feet and I are getting on the first flight we can get tomorrow and then you're mine."

A relieved-sounding sigh escaped Bay. "I love the sound of that last part."

The dark and controlling bastard inside Antonio grew larger. "Me too. Are you mine, Bay?"

"I believe I am." The way he answered without hesitation had Antonio's pride swelling.

"You won't regret me."

"I know. I don't believe in regret," Bay tacked on with a chuckle. "Every choice I've made in my life has been exactly that, my choice. Maybe things worked out. Maybe they didn't. Either way, it's on me. I'm choosing you."

"Damn. I can't wait to be with you again."

"Go to sleep," Bay ordered. "Cuddle up with Sparkle Feet and dream of me. The quicker you fall asleep, the faster we can be together."

A warmth spread through Antonio's chest. He hadn't felt this way before. "Okay, but only if you go home and stop working yourself into the ground for the night."

"Deal." Bay's features softened, making Antonio desperate to kiss him. "Goodnight, Sparkle Feet, and you too, sexy angel."

Antonio sucked in a breath around the emotions that had him in a chokehold. *"Buona notte, amore mio."*

Long after Bay's image disappeared from the screen, Antonio kept staring at his phone while lost in thought. Bay lived over three hundred miles away. Antonio wondered what he was doing. Maybe this was a waste of time. The problem was, he felt something. Antonio didn't feel things. Not for anyone and not for lack of trying. Derreck was right. This one was very different. Antonio couldn't stop until he found out why.

FOUR

It wasn't until Antonio stood in the back parking lot of the casino that the fear started setting in. Could he do this? Lombardi Casino was his haven. Maybe he didn't even have what it took to be in a real relationship that existed outside his comfort zone. Fuck. What if he got to Arizona and Bay changed his mind?

"Did you take your meds?"

Antonio dragged himself from the edge of panic to focus on Derreck. The man's oddly colored amber eyes were as familiar as his own and steadied Antonio in his moment of need. "Yes. Two Xanax, a blood thinner, and my blood pressure meds, as ordered."

Derreck didn't look appeased. "What about your vitamins?"

"I'm taking them tonight before bed." Sometimes Derreck made him feel like a little kid, but really, Antonio needed a keeper. "So you packed all your bottles, right? Do I need to swing by the pharmacy before taking you to the airport or are you good?"

Antonio fought the urge to growl. "I'm good. Everything was refilled last week."

Derreck's gaze moved over Antonio's face. "Are you sure you want to do this? There won't be anyone watching out for you in Phoenix."

In times like these, Antonio truly realized how far he had fallen. "Bay is a doctor and I'm not an invalid. It'll be fine." Antonio took Derreck's hand and brought it to his lips. "I swear." They had known each other too long. No doubt Derreck knew Antonio's game—that he used his charms to get his way.

Derreck snorted and pulled his hand away. "All right, Romeo. Go, try to win this man, but if you need me, I'm only a phone call away. You know I'll be there. Whatever it takes. Even if I have to drive all night."

"I know." He really did. Derreck was a good man. He deserved a break from Antonio's bullshit.

"Think of this as a vacation. You're free to do whatever without worrying what's going on with me. Hell, this is your chance, take a vacation. Go to the beach."

"Take a look at my gorgeous black skin," Derreck deadpanned, as if Antonio didn't see him every day. "This magnificence," he said, waving toward his face, "sunburns and then gets darker. You know I don't hang out on the beach."

Antonio rolled his eyes. He knew Derreck was being ridiculous on his behalf. "We've been to the beach together, so that's some bullshit."

Derreck's deep-sounding laughter washed over Antonio as Antonio gathered his bags. "You chose that destination. I just wanted to go to Disney." Derreck kept up the chatter while Antonio focused on his thoughts. It was only an hour flight from Vegas to Phoenix, but his meds would likely knock him out soon. It was a private flight from a small airstrip, so he wouldn't likely encounter many people. His discomfort wouldn't get too out of control until he reached Phoenix. Even then, he should be okay. A driver would meet him, and they probably wouldn't chitchat. As long as Antonio kept taking deep breaths, he would be fine. That was what he kept telling himself.

In truth, Antonio didn't breathe a sigh of relief until he reached Phoenix and was settled in the backseat of a nondescript black SUV. Unfortunately, the driver wasn't as quiet as Antonio hoped.

"What brings you to town, business or pleasure?"

"Pleasure. I'm visiting a friend." Antonio kept his voice bland, expecting his tone would deter any further conversation. It wasn't to be.

"Where are you from originally? I can't place the accent."

Antonio drew a slow breath in through his nose. "Florence. Italy," he expounded, in case the dark-haired man hadn't passed maps in school. Antonio had never been great at geography himself.

"Oh, nice. I've never been there myself, but I've seen images online. How long have you been stateside?"

"A very long time." Antonio wasn't trying to be vague. He simply didn't want to chat.

"I get that. I'm originally from Vermont and I can't even recall how long I've been in Arizona. Time gets away from you. Do you have anything fun planned while you're here? We have some awesome golf courses and Vegas-style casinos, if you're into that sort of thing."

Antonio bit back a laugh. His phone rang, saving

him. "Ah. Excuse me." He answered before Mr. Chat All Day could respond. "Hello?"

"Hello, gorgeous. How was your flight?"

Antonio dropped his gaze to his lap to hide his smile. "It was good. I'm on my way to your place now."

"We're about two minutes away," the driver said, interjecting.

Antonio passed the information along. "Two minutes away."

"Yay. I wish I was off work today. I'm ready to see you."

"It's fine." Antonio still needed to sleep off the high dose of anxiety meds. "This gives me a chance to snoop through your things."

A sexy chuckle caressed his ear, making Antonio's eyes fall closed. "Let me know when you're there and I can unlock the door from my phone."

Antonio glanced up and took in his surroundings. It was a nice neighborhood. Expensive homes locked behind huge fences lined the street. The car turned down the driveway of a white stone house. It was large and beautiful. "I believe we're here."

"Great. I'm unlocking the door and shutting down the alarm as we speak."

Antonio dug out his wallet as the driver slipped from the vehicle and opened the back to grab Antonio's bags. He pulled out some money for a tip before exiting. He met the driver at the back, passed along the money, and took control of his bags. He flashed the guy a smile with the phone wedged between his shoulder and ear. With a nod, the guy left him in peace. Antonio dragged his suitcases to the door.

"Headed inside now." The door easily swung inward beneath Antonio's hand. Antonio's eyebrows crawled toward his hairline at the sight meeting him. Everything was white and bright. Clean and crisp. The place was perfectly styled and looked like no one lived there. It was like a show home. "Damn, Bay. This is a nice place."

"Thank you. If you head to your right and down the hall, the first room on the left is my bedroom. Make yourself at home."

Antonio followed Bay's directions into a space that smelled like Bay's cologne. One wall looked to be all French doors, leading to a pool. The bed was high and huge with deep maroon bedding. Antonio dragged his bags to the edge of a bench at the foot of the bed and sat. Now that he was here, his shoulders relaxed, and he realized how tired he was from the strain. "Your bed looks comfy."

"You should try it out." Bay's voice turned sultry. "Take a nap. Get acquainted with the place. Reserve your energy."

He couldn't stop smiling at the happiness in Bay's voice. "Sounds like a plan. I can't wait to see you."

"Same. I have to get back to work, but I promise to hurry."

"Don't worry about me. I'm not going anywhere." Antonio was in Bay's home now. Bay didn't stand a chance. Antonio planned to lay siege to his life. Bay was as good as locked down. He was one hundred percent off the market.

―――――――

IT HAD BEEN A LONG DAMN TIME SINCE BAY made it through work as fast as he did today. He tried not to appear as desperate to be home as he was, but Antonio waited. Damn, just the thought of that had Bay smiling like an idiot all day. They had spent a single weekend together and already Bay was a mess over Antonio. In his heart, he knew Antonio was too good to be true. All the knowledge in the world couldn't save Bay. He was beyond ready for another beautiful man to wreck him.

The smell of cooking food overwhelmed Bay as he came through the door. His steps slowed. He couldn't recall the last time he came home to a meal. Bay dumped his stuff by the door and headed for the kitchen. His heart sped at the sight of Antonio chopping vegetables at the island. In a t-shirt and jeans, and with his hair a mess, Antonio looked sexier than any man Bay had ever seen. Bay didn't think it had a damn thing to do with Antonio's appearance. It was Bay. He was bewitched.

Antonio glanced up, catching sight of him. His face lit. "Hey. I didn't hear you come in."

Goddamn. That sexy Italian accent got him every time. It hit him in the gut. "What's all this?" Bay asked, crossing the room. "I mean, I'm intrigued, and my mouth is already watering, but I thought you're supposed be my guest."

With a shrug, Antonio set his knife aside and swiped his hands on his pants. "You looked so tired when we talked last night. I wanted to help you relax."

Bay invaded Antonio's space. "Don't worry. I got

plenty of sleep." He moved even closer, sliding his hands across Antonio's hips.

Antonio snagged the collar of Bay's shirt. "Good. You'll need it," Antonio warned as he claimed Bay's mouth. Lust exploded inside Bay. Antonio's ass filled Bay's hands and he squeezed before he realized he planned to do so. He didn't stop. Bay hauled Antonio closer, rocking against him and letting him feel Bay's desire as their tongues clashed. His mind was already a mess. Antonio's fingers dug into Bay's jaw as he shoved Bay's head back, exposing his throat. Bay gasped for air while Antonio nipped and sucked at his neck. It was like Antonio knew every button to push to make Bay as hot as possible. Already set to boil, Bay fought the urge to drop to his knees. He could make Antonio scream his name.

Antonio's lips softened against Bay's throat until they barely brushed his skin. "You're probably ready for a shower." Antonio's whispered words caressed Bay, making goosebumps run down his spine. "Do what you need, and I'll finish dinner." He forced Bay's lips back to his while still holding Bay's jaw in a tight grip. Antonio barely brushed his lips across Bay's. "Change into something comfortable. You won't be wearing it long."

Bay's cock twitched at the threat. A pant burst

from Bay's chest. His body followed Antonio's orders on autopilot—like Antonio controlled him by remote. He took a step back, but his head refused to budge. His mouth chased after Antonio. Bay stole one more kiss before turning away. He already knew this would be the fastest shower in history.

In the bedroom, he found Sparkle Feet sitting on his bed. He had a new friend. A light blue unicorn with human-looking eyes and a golden horn cuddled Sparkle Feet. Bay picked him up and inspected him. He had a rainbow tail. With a chuckle, Bay put the unicorn back where it had been, cuddling his sparkle-footed companion. He headed for the shower. As he fired the water to life, he caught sight of himself in the mirror. A huge smile stretched his lips. He hadn't realized he had been smiling while by himself like a complete lunatic. It was nice. Bay had forgotten what it was like to be genuinely happy. He ignored the fact that he had also been semi-hard since the moment he met Antonio.

Bay rushed through his shower before finding a pair of shorts that had once been sweats. Honestly, he kind of looked like a hobo after throwing on the first set of comfortable clothes he could find. Bay didn't give a shit about any of that. Antonio was waiting. By the time he made it back to the kitchen,

Bay measured each step to stop himself from running. Antonio stood at the counter where Bay left him. He glanced up as Bay cleared the doorway. His gaze traveled down Bay's body and back up again. The heat in Antonio's stare had Bay fighting a pant.

"You're just in time. Everything is ready."

Bay's stomach growled. He had a feeling it had nothing to do with hunger for food. "It smells delicious. What's on the menu?"

"Mushroom risotto."

"Healthy and delicious," Bay said, still fighting the urge to tackle Antonio to the floor. "Tomorrow night, I'll take you to my favorite restaurant. You shouldn't have to cook. This is your vacation."

Antonio pulled a pained smile as he grabbed two plates. "If that's what you'd like."

Guilt immediately set in. He had forgotten about Antonio's anxiety issues, but this was the perfect opening for Bay to find out more. "When I was in Vegas, you said you used to play golf. Do you mind if I ask what changed in your life? I mean, it doesn't sound like you've always been introverted."

Antonio chuckled. "Introverted. That sounds so much better than batshit crazy."

"You're not crazy." Bay said the words with the confidence of his profession. Something always triggered these changes in mental health. Antonio wasn't crazy. Plus, Bay didn't like that word. It was disrespectful to people who suffered from things they couldn't control.

Antonio's smile slipped away. He focused on the task of fixing their plates, openly avoiding Bay's stare. "I had a stroke." The words took Bay by surprise, but Antonio didn't pause and give him time to react. "For many years, I lived the lifestyle of a single, wealthy casino owner. I drank, partied, and my blood pressure was out of control. Since I was convinced I was invincible, I also never went to the doctor. At thirty-five, while sitting at a Craps table and living life to its fullest, I had a stroke."

Bay eyed him for all the obvious signs. There were none that he could see. "Wow. You obviously got really lucky if you're standing here to tell about it."

When Antonio's chin lifted and his gaze finally focused on Bay, Bay had to take a slow breath at Antonio's intensity. Sometimes, he was almost frightening. His emotions were thicker than most people's. They blanketed Bay. Antonio motioned absently toward his left eye. "I'm almost completely blind in this eye now. But yes, I got very lucky." Antonio went back to his task while he spoke. "At first, when I didn't want to do any of the things I used to do, I chalked it up to still recovering. Then, I noticed that when people would approach me from my left side and startle me, my heart would race out of control. I would shake and have to sit down. Each time it happened, it seemed to take me longer to recover afterward. Still, I thought those episodes would stop once I adjusted to losing half my vision." A sad-looking smile touched Antonio's lips. "Instead, things got worse. It seemed like the smallest things overwhelmed me. Derreck had to start shadowing me everywhere I went in case I suddenly couldn't breathe."

It hit Bay. Derreck had been in the background the entire weekend. Bay hadn't thought anything of it. He just assumed Derreck had been working. "He's good at his job. I didn't realize he was watching over you."

Antonio passed him a plate and snagged his own. He motioned toward the kitchen table, continuing with his story as they moved to sit. "We've been friends a long time. I don't know how I would've survived without him. Anyhow, that's basically it. I stopped feeling safe anywhere except the casino. Even then, I usually have a book with me for the moments I need to escape everyone's eyes. If I do go out, it's easier if I have someone with me, so I can focus on them rather than my surroundings. Most people can't take the over-the-top neediness of being with me now, which I get. When I'm uncomfortable, I act ridiculous to hide the fact that I'm uncomfortable, but I also know I'm being ridiculous, which only makes things worse. It's a vicious cycle that makes it even harder to endure my company. Somewhere along the way, I stopped trying. You're smiling."

Bay realized Antonio was right. He was smiling. "None of those things stopped you from approaching me."

Antonio's mouth lifted in one corner. "I said I have panic attacks. I didn't say I'm an idiot."

Bay swore even his heart sighed. He needed to give as much of himself as Antonio offered with his confessions. "I'm awkward and always tell too much of my business when I get uncomfortable. If you'd be willing to try, I'd love to go places with you and let you focus completely on me while being as ridiculous as possible. In fact, I would love to see that side of you."

With a small shake of his head, Antonio visibly fought a smile. "Sure. Whatever keeps you smiling. Now, tell me about your day."

Something deep and powerful settled over Bay as he fell into a story about his day and the antics of two of his nurses. This was the life he wanted. Quiet. Calm. A slight hum of lust lingering beneath every moment, waiting to burst to life. Maybe, to anyone else, this might seem unexciting. Bay was an adult. He wanted something real and lasting. Antonio felt like he could be the one.

ANTONIO COULDN'T STOP STARING AT BAY'S mouth. He caught himself biting his lip as he watched the way Bay's jaw worked and tore his gaze away. Fuck. Bay was sexy. He chewed his lip again. Antonio took a breath and tried to make himself stop.

"You're an amazing cook. Every time I learn something new about you, I'm blown away all over again that no one has locked you down."

"You're beautiful." Even Antonio heard the hunger in his voice.

Bay blushed. His gaze slid away.

Antonio's possessiveness grew. He leaned closer and slid his hand up the inside of Bay's thigh. "I'm being serious. You make it hard for me to focus, but I also want to know every tiny detail about your life. It's a predicament, to be sure."

Demure Bay vanished. He boldly held Antonio's stare. "I think you should fuck me and then maybe you can concentrate again."

The instant longing took Antonio's breath. Everything about Antonio hardened. His response to Bay's dare was every bit as mental as it was physical. He didn't possess a passive nature when it came to relationships. Antonio was controlling and intense. He liked to addict people to his touch. His hand moved higher up Bay's thigh. He let his fingertips skim the erection tenting Bay's shorts. His stomach muscles clenched with desire. Antonio snagged his wine glass and polished off his drink before standing and holding his hand out to Bay.

Bay came to his feet. Their fingers linked. Together, they made their way down the hall to Bay's bedroom. Even once they were there, they didn't fall on each other—crazed. Bay picked up the unicorn Antonio had ordered as a friend for Sparkle Feet.

"I see we have a new addition. Is Sparkle Feet excited to have company?"

Antonio winked as he peeled off his shirt. "Rainbow Tail is the perfect companion. He's masculine but not oppressive. I think if Sparkle Feet plays his cards right, they might have a beautiful life together."

Bay's gaze moved down Antonio's body. "Is that so?"

"Yes." He crowded Bay's space and went to work on stealing his clothes. "I feel like I've been waiting forever to have you. That sounds unreasonable, I know." His gaze met Bay's. "But that's how I feel." Antonio knew he probably looked as intense and possessive as he felt. It was out of his control.

Bay didn't look scared. The opposite, in fact. He looked entranced. "I know I've been waiting forever for you. I just didn't know that I was waiting."

Antonio froze with Bay's shirt lifted halfway up his torso. Each and every time he thought to wow Bay, Bay was the one who ended up stealing Antonio's heart. Thoughts about being inside Bay floated away. Being with Bay became about more than flying high. Antonio kissed him. The way their tongues brushed was more than sweet. Their kiss was almost reverent. It wasn't until cool air brushed his ass that Antonio realized Bay's hands had been busy. Then, Bay's fingers encircled Antonio's erection and Antonio's knees nearly buckled. Bay obviously didn't intend to be passive. Antonio needed to get moving if he didn't want to blow in Bay's hand.

Antonio hardened his heart against his instant need to come and pulled away. "Strip." While Bay did as ordered, Antonio finished undressing and moved to grab the lube and condoms he had brought with him. He suited up and oiled himself while Bay watched. Antonio stroked himself, watching the hunger grow in Bay's eyes. "Get on the bed, Bay. I have plans for you."

Bay scrambled to do as told, proving how hot he was for Antonio. As he settled onto his back, Bay's cock stood proud and waiting. Antonio's mouth watered at the sight. He crawled his way up Bay's body, stopping only long enough to suck Bay's dick and make him writhe. When he pulled away, Bay looked half crazed, but he didn't make a sound. Antonio couldn't have that. He needed Bay to scream.

Antonio urged Bay onto his stomach. "Roll over, sexy. I want to play with that ass." With Bay's sexy round ass exposed, Antonio bit his cheek. When Bay moaned, Antonio's desperation grew. He urged Bay onto his knees, exposing him to Antonio's every whim. Antonio bit the other cheek before slapping Bay's ass with both hands and spreading him wide. A whimper escaped Antonio at the first sight of Bay's waiting asshole.

"Goddamn, *amore mio*. You are begging for me. I can't resist you." He leaned in and licked Bay's asshole. Bay made a sound of longing that nearly caved Antonio's chest. His dick leaked inside the condom, pleading with Antonio to take Bay hard. Instead, he chose to torment himself and tongue Bay's hole. He probed and licked until Bay squirmed and begged. Only when he thought his mind might snap did Antonio shoot upward and impale Bay. A loud cry rent the air. Antonio no longer knew who made which sound. It took a second of Bay's tight ass violently sucking him deeper for Antonio to realize Bay had come. His mind was too big of a mess to comprehend the magnitude of the moment. Bay had been so hot and impatient for him that he had barely withstood them joining. Antonio was right there with him. Three trusts in and Antonio was pumping the condom full of cum. His entire body shook from the overwhelming moment. He was damn glad Bay had been every bit as over enthusiastic as him. Otherwise, he might have disappointed Bay. Hell, he wasn't sure he hadn't somewhat let the man down. Antonio had never blown so hard and fast in his life. Even his first time hadn't ended this quickly.

Antonio panted against Bay's spine as they collapsed together. "I'm sorry, angel. I don't think I realized how hard being with you would hit me. It's not usual for me to be so quick to finish."

Bay's body shook with laughter. "I think we both were a little over excited. But I have zero regrets. Jesus. My skin is still on fire."

Antonio let his cock slip from Bay's ass before urging Bay to roll over. The moment he could, Antonio claimed Bay's lips. They kissed slow and sweet—the way they should have made love. Next time, Antonio swore. He would go slow and savor every second. They had time. Antonio wasn't going anywhere. He would make Bay proud. Bay would see. Antonio had lots of tricks left up his sleeve. He would make Bay proud.

FIVE

THE OUTLINE OF ANOTHER BODY FILLING HIS BED was a welcome sight. Bay had turned off his alarm ten minutes ago. He needed to get up, but his body wouldn't budge. There was a sexy man in his bed. Bay's heart couldn't take it. He couldn't move. Without thought, he found himself slithering closer. If he skipped his morning workout, he could spend a little longer with Antonio before work.

Last night had been amazing. It seemed a little ridiculous for him to be so blown away, because he had never come in one thrust like that in his entire life. In fact, Bay was a little embarrassed about it, but damn. Antonio had gotten him hotter faster than anyone in his life had ever done. He had been shameless. Antonio had ensured Bay couldn't doubt how wanted he was, and it had been sexy as sin. Bay needed Antonio to know he was every bit as desired.

Bay ducked beneath the covers, moving slow. He didn't want Antonio to be too awake. Bay only needed Antonio lucid enough to orgasm. Thankfully, they had slept nude. It was easy to settle in close to Antonio and get to work. The moment his lips locked around Antonio's soft cock, Antonio buried his fingers in Bay's hair.

"*Oddio*, Bay." The whispered exclamation had Bay's chest filling with pride. He didn't normally feel like he was very good at pleasing anyone. Antonio made him feel like he could take over the world.

Bay put his heart into sucking Antonio. Antonio whimpered and squirmed beneath him, reaching for release. Bay's dick twitched with desire, but this wasn't about him. He could always jack off in the shower. Bay was used to handling things alone. His pleasure didn't matter all that much.

In a flurry of motion, Bay found himself on his back with Antonio straddling his face and his cock in Antonio's mouth. In his surprise, Bay didn't react right away. He passively allowed Antonio to fuck his throat while he tried to figure out how he had ended up in this position. Then, the ecstasy set in. Antonio did some flick of the tongue thing that had Bay's eyes rolling back in his head. He couldn't let Antonio be disappointed. Bay sucked and swallowed while his hips lifted, seeking more of Antonio's talented mouth. The closer Antonio dragged him toward the edge, the harder Bay worked to please him. A strangled cry vibrated around Bay's cock. Cum filled Bay's mouth. Bay's dick slipped down Antonio's throat while Antonio pulled some trick that made Bay's entire body spasm as he came. He nearly choked on Antonio's cum when his mind stopped working. Pleasure rocked his entire body. Bay swore he levitated for a moment.

Antonio settled back down in his spot next to Bay while Bay gasped for air. Once again, he was the one left a gibbering mess. He wished he didn't have to work. Bay wanted to stay put until he actually came out on top. It seemed he would have to keep trying. This definitely settled one debate Bay had been having with himself. He would take some time off and dedicate his full attention to Antonio. Bay couldn't handle Antonio while running half strength. Someone as perfect as Antonio deserved to be Bay's sole focus.

His gaze moved Antonio's way. Antonio was already asleep again while Bay's mind was a mess.

He would settle things at work today and then Antonio wouldn't know what hit him. Bay wouldn't stop until they were set in stone.

BEING ALONE ALL DAY IN BAY'S HOUSE GAVE Antonio plenty of time to make plans to steal Bay's heart. By the time Bay made it home and got out of the shower, Antonio was practically dancing in place outside the bathroom door, ready to play.

A sexy laugh rumbled from Bay when he opened the bathroom door. "Have you been standing there the whole time?"

"Sorry. I have a surprise for you."

Bay shook his head as he invaded Antonio's space. "Don't apologize. You're adorable and I missed you today. I'm feeling like you missed me too."

Antonio swore his heart sighed as he melted. "Si. Yes. Very much." His hands automatically slid up the sexy pecs he loved so much as Bay lowered his head. Their lips met and Antonio lost himself for a moment. Only the reminder of what waited inside one of Bay's many empty bedrooms had Antonio taking a step back. "Come on, gorgeous. Your surprise is waiting."

"I love surprises, but I swear you do too much. Having you here is enough for me."

"We'll have plenty of quiet nights at home," Antonio promised over his shoulder. "But tonight, you must accept my fun time."

"I'll try to survive it."

Antonio fought a laugh at Bay's fake put upon tone. As they cleared the doorway into the spare room, Bay stopped. He eyed the gift boxes with holes cut in the top that Antonio had arranged into three rows and three boxes deep. "What's this?"

"It's surprise fun time." He grabbed a palm-sized bean bag and handed it Bay's way. "Toss it and whichever box it lands in, you have to open and we have to play with whatever is inside. No arguments. It is a twist on the strange corn hole game some people enjoy so much."

The smile Bay wore said it all. He loved the idea. "What's inside?"

Antonio fought a knowing grin. "You will see."

With a chuckle, Bay tossed the bag toward one of the biggest gifts. It went skidding across the lid before dropping inside. "Damn. I can't believe I made that."

"Go open it," Antonio said, slapping Bay's ass and sending him on his way. While Bay crossed the room and grabbed the gift, Antonio moved to the empty side of the room. He already knew what was inside, so he sat on the floor to get ready to play.

Bay joined him on the floor before lifting the lid on the box. A bright smile exploded across Bay's face. "A train set. Oh my god. This is awesome."

Antonio helped him take out the pieces. "You said the only time you can recall your dad having any time for you was when you built trains and miniatures together."

"I can't believe you thought of this. That was a passing comment while we talked all day in Vegas. That's such a small detail to remember."

"Maybe so, but I was listening. You'll have to show me how to do this. I've never put together a train set."

Bay moved close and dumped out the rest of the pieces. "It's pretty simple." He handed Antonio different parts while explaining how each one fit together. Antonio listened only enough to follow Bay's instructions. The rest of his brain focused on simply being with Bay. He savored the cadence of Bay's voice. The way their knees and elbows kept brushing held him fascinated. Antonio was happy. It wasn't that life had been stale before Bay. Antonio always found company one way or another. This was different. He wasn't passing time with Bay. They were building something more than a train set, which they had done in a matter of minutes. Thankfully, Antonio had thought to also order batteries because the toy took a ton. While Bay popped the batteries in, Antonio stared at Bay's profile. They were building a life. Antonio felt it in his gut.

Bay smiled as he fired the train to life. He watched it go around the track once before looking Antonio's way, catching him staring. Bay didn't call him on it. "How do you always do so much for me?"

Antonio shrugged. "Everywhere delivers these days, so it's not hard to get whatever I need."

With a dismissive motion, Bay swiped away Antonio's explanation. "That's not what I meant." He motioned toward the pile of gifts still waiting. "How do you come up with these ideas and blow me away the way you do? Do people really do amazing things like this?"

"I don't know," Antonio answered honestly. "All I know is that I have to make you smile. It's almost a desperation inside me. You should throw the bag again."

Bay overcame him, knocking him to the floor. A

burst of surprised laughter escaped Antonio as Bay covered Antonio's body with his. Bay captured his mouth and swallowed the sound. As quickly as it happened, it was over. Bay crawled away and dropped the bag into the closest box. Before Antonio could cry foul for the obvious cheating at the game, Bay was already opening the box. His face made Antonio staying quiet worthwhile.

Bay pulled a double-sided dildo and a bottle of lube from the box. He visibly tried rearranging his features to hide his shock. "Oh. Okay." His shoulders squared and he met Antonio's gaze. "Do you know, I've never used one of these."

"What?" Even Antonio heard the surprise in his tone.

Bay shrugged. "Matty wasn't... never mind. I guess I need to learn to stop saying his name."

Antonio fought an eye roll. "You two were married. It's fine. He was a huge chunk of your life. Now explain. How have you never done this? We're not sixteen."

A blush touched Bay's cheeks as he squirmed beneath Antonio's question. "Matty wasn't very adventurous. He kind of liked what he liked, and we did what got him off. Otherwise, we never tried anything new."

That wasn't good enough. Antonio still couldn't wrap his mind around it. "You speak as if Matty is the only man you've ever been with and you had no choice in the matter. I cannot accept that."

Bay looked even more uncomfortable and wouldn't meet Antonio's stare. "Well, I mean, we started dating in high school and then we got married. Since we split, I've only been on a couple of dates and those didn't really pan out." Antonio was completely flabbergasted. Bay stared at a spot over Antonio's shoulder. When he spoke again, he sounded defeated. "Maybe I'm the boring one." Bay's gaze finally slid his way. "It's very possible I'm the one who's always been unwilling to try something new."

Antonio shook his head. He couldn't believe how blind Bay could be. "You're not boring. You're loyal. I think it's beautiful. You dedicated your life to someone who gave you nothing and thought of you not at all. I do nothing but think of you." He stood and peeled off his shirt. "You should strip, gorgeous. The days of trying nothing new are over. I'm all the adventure you'll ever need."

Bay came to his feet. He slowly undressed while Antonio watched. The moment he was nude, Antonio sat and crooked his finger, beckoning Bay closer. Once Bay stood over him, Antonio's hands immediately ran up Bay's legs. He squeezed and massaged, drawing Bay even closer. Antonio shifted positions, moving to his knees. With his gaze locked on Bay's semi-hard cock, Antonio leaned in and licked before dragging Bay's rapidly hardening dick into his mouth. He sucked. A moan bounced off the walls. Bay swayed on his feet. His fingers dug into Antonio's hair and hung on. Antonio closed his eyes and savored the moment. He felt so much. Too much for someone he just met. He couldn't stop.

Antonio's gaze flipped upward. Bay stared down at him with flushed cheeks and his heart in his eyes. Hope filled Antonio until he thought he might burst. He pulled away and kissed Bay's thigh.

"Sit."

At Antonio's order, Bay dropped to the floor. Antonio had a hard time looking anywhere else but at Bay's saliva-covered cock. It begged for more and Antonio wanted to give everything. But he wasn't Matty. Bay needed to see there was more to the world than getting sucked and fucked. There intimacy in adventure. Heated looks kept passing between them as Antonio lubed both ends of the dildo. Bay's cheeks were flushed, and his eyes shone bright with lust. Antonio couldn't resist him.

"You're incredibly gorgeous. Impossible to resist, really." Antonio kept up the praise as he urged Bay to lean back on his elbows, spread his knees, and let Antonio in. "It's insane to me that you haven't had men beating down your door and begging to stick things in this sexy round ass." He teased Bay's asshole with the wet toy, swiping it back and forth until Bay's knees fell open and he moved restlessly. Then, Antonio slipped the tip inside. "Your body is greedy for it. Do you feel the way you're sucking this toy deeper? How have you denied this body all the joy it screams for? It's almost like you've been waiting for me."

Antonio kissed Bay's chest. He moved lower and sucked Bay's dick for a moment longer before finally sitting between Bay's knees. He scooted as close as he could get before draping his legs over Bay's thighs. Once in position, he worked the other end of the toy inside his ass. Antonio sucked in a hiss as the dildo filled him. He had always been a sexual person. Even when he didn't have a partner, Antonio didn't deny himself. He loved orgasms and dragging out the building pleasure before release. Antonio owned a treasure trove of toys. He loved filling his ass with the prefect weight and size of pulsing and vibrating things while another toy milked his hard dick.

Sometimes, when the anxiety took hold and there was no other relief, Antonio would stay in bed and writhe with pleasure to drown out the rest of life. Everything was better with a partner, though. As he went ass to ass with Bay, a low moan ripped from his throat. There was no replacing the warmth of another human.

"Oh, god." Antonio blindly reached for Bay's hand. Their fingers linked and Antonio threw his head back and gasped as he rocked on the toy and Bay did the same. He lifted his hips and pushed against Bay and the toy. Their asses flexed against one another. Antonio's dick leaked on his stomach. He fed on every sensation and sound.

"Goddamn, Nino. You're killing me. I've never seen anyone look so turned on." Bay only rambled, yet Antonio hung on every breathless word. He knew he had Bay in the realest place he could be. Bay rode that plane where the most honest words he ever spoke fell from his lips. Antonio wanted all of his confessions. Bay gave them. "All my life, I've been a bottom with no desire to be inside anyone, but I want to fuck you right now so I can taste your lips while you writhe like you are with this toy in your ass. Goddamn, I want to be the toy in your ass."

Antonio couldn't take Bay's teasing words any

longer. He pushed the toy away, leaving it inside Bay, and he quickly straddled Bay's body. He might not ever have Bay this mindless again. Antonio loved getting fucked every bit as much as he loved having his cock buried in a tight ass. Before Bay could change his mind, Antonio was on his dick. His asshole was full of lube thanks to the dildo and more than ready. Still, Bay wasn't a small guy. Antonio growled at the fullness.

He was out of his head with lust. Mindlessly, he ate at Bay's mouth, sucking and licking as he bounced on Bay's lap. He took everything he wanted. His cock kissed Bay's torso with every bounce. The friction had Antonio moaning around Bay's tongue. Bay's arms locked around him. He thrust upward, slamming inside Antonio, taking his pleasure from Antonio's body. Antonio held his breath. His entire body clenched before a spasm made his whole body jerk with ecstasy. Bay tore his mouth away and bit Antonio's shoulder. He cried out against Antonio's skin. The moment felt powerful. Even as he still shook and gasped in Bay's arms, Antonio knew he had just taken Bay somewhere he had never been before. He felt like a god. No one had ever gotten him so high. He wanted more. Needed more. Antonio needed forever. Fuck. Realization struck like lightning. Bay was the one.

As Bay slowly came down from the mind-bending journey Antonio had taken him on, the reality of the moment set in. He had just made love to Antonio sans condom and no discussion on the matter. While, granted, he had only been with one other man in his life, Bay still should have known better. He was a doctor. Being healthy was important to him. But fuck him, that had been amazing. No one, not one damn soul on this planet had ever made him feel the way he did now. They needed to talk, but Bay couldn't stop kissing Antonio. He couldn't loosen his arms and let Antonio get away. It was too soon. Way, way too early in their relationship, but Bay couldn't deny the emotions slamming against his mind. Amazing sex and new experiences aside, Bay was falling in love. It was like Antonio cast a spell. He had Bay enraptured. That was why Bay had to keep him safe.

He swiped a light kiss across Antonio's lips and then kissed the tip of his nose. "We didn't use a condom."

With his eyes closed and still gasping for air, Antonio was a beautiful mess. His skin was flushed. His lips were swollen. Bay wanted him again. "I'm sorry." His eyes opened. Those sexy blue irises that had captured Bay's heart stared at him. "That's my fault. I got carried away."

Bay shook his head. His lips automatically sought more kisses before he could respond. "I wanted you. Nothing else mattered in the moment. I have to be tested for everything all the time as part of my profession. You don't have anything to fear from me, but I still feel incredibly guilty for not talking to you about it first."

Antonio shushed him as he claimed Bay's mouth again. Their bodies were still connected. Bay questioned if he felt as much guilt as he claimed, considering he wasn't exactly trying to stop. In fact, it felt damn good being inside Antonio, the heat still slightly sucking him had Bay's cock twitching with aftershocks.

Antonio licked Bay's upper lip in a sexy way Bay had never experienced. The move had him chasing Antonio's mouth. "My last partner cheated, and I got tested as soon as I found out, even though we were always safe. Everything came back negative. I think we are fine." He kissed the corner of Bay's mouth, still seducing him. "Plus, I can't regret this. In fact, I can't even move. My cum is drying between us and I can feel your dick twitching in my ass. Fuck, Bay. Don't you feel it?" Bay felt all those things, but he wasn't sure that was what Antonio meant. Antonio kept sucking Bay's tongue, as if he didn't expect a response. He pulled away just enough to press his forehead to Bay's. His gaze was too close and intense for Bay to look anywhere else. "I know you have to feel it," Antonio said, confirming his thoughts about there being more to Antonio's claim. "We were meant to meet. This is too perfect to be chance." Antonio whispered the words, somehow making them even more powerful.

Bay held on to Antonio. He couldn't let go. "I feel it."

A smile exploded across Antonio's face at Bay's confession. He captured Bay's mouth, saving him from saying more and embarrassing himself. He rolled, pinning Antonio to the floor. The dildo slipped from Bay's ass and hit the floor in a loud plop. Laughter vibrated through their kiss, but they didn't stop. Bay had never been this happy. He didn't know people could feel this way. It was time for him to go all in with Antonio. If there was ever anyone worth risking another heart break for, it was the man currently getting him hard again. No one had ever made him so hot for life. He had a boner for happiness. Bay was horny for a future with Antonio. Laughter filled his soul. He wanted to fuck until his dick was raw. Antonio had created a monster.

SIX

AFTER A FEW WEEKS OFF AND DOING NOTHING but focusing on his budding romance with Antonio, Bay knew one thing with absolute certainty. He was completely in love with Antonio. While Antonio constantly challenged him, forcing him to try new things and play with him, Bay pushed Antonio out of his comfort zone. That was why they were eating at Bay's favorite restaurant tonight.

Each time Bay had tried taking Antonio on a real date, Antonio had found a way to thwart him. Usually, he seduced Bay into staying in for the night. While Bay was fine with that, he also wanted Antonio to feel comfortable going a few places in Phoenix. Otherwise, he didn't know how to convince Antonio to stay permanently. Tonight, Antonio would be the one seduced if it was the last thing Bay did.

Bay chose a booth in the back corner of the restaurant. He let Antonio have the side facing the wall, so no one could see him. He also ordered for them, keeping Antonio from having to interact with anyone. Once they were alone, they reached for each other at the same time. Their fingers linked across the table. Bay smiled as they toyed with each other's hand. A globed candle on the table had tiny orange lights dancing in Antonio's eyes. The low lighting and soft music that played set the mood. Bay swore the air was thick with desire. The way Antonio held his stare screamed that Bay would get fucked later. There was always an underlying heat between them. Without any words spoken, their feelings were out there for anyone to see. Sometimes, Bay wondered which of them would break first. Maybe neither of them would. It was possible they both knew there didn't seem to be a middle ground with them. One of them would have to give up everything if they wanted to be together. No one wanted to be the first to say that aloud.

With Bay lost in thought, their food appeared between them.

Their tiny blonde waitress looked frazzled. "Sorry about your wait."

"Are you saying I'm fat?"

Bay bit his lip at not only Antonio's immediate and ridiculous response, but the waitress's face. "He's joking," Bay said, stepping in before the poor girl started stammering. He thanked her for them both, hoping to spare Antonio any further discomfort. As much as he adored Antonio's humor when he was distressed, Bay didn't want him to be uncomfortable. Bay stood and spoke quietly to the waitress before she got away. "There's a two-hundred-dollar tip in it for you if you don't come back to check on us for ten minutes."

She was a true professional who had seen everything, because she didn't as much as blink. "You got it."

Bay swapped sides, forcing Antonio to make room for him on his side of the booth. "I'll sit here. That way, no one can sneak up on you again."

Antonio flashed him a smile. "Sorry."

Bay couldn't beat back the happiness. "Don't apologize. I think you're adorable." If there was one thing Bay knew, it was that anxiety didn't always look the way people expected. Sometimes, it was ridiculous dad jokes with waitresses. Right now, though, Bay was about to find out what Antonio's anxiety looked like while getting jacked off in public.

He dragged the table closer so Antonio's lap would be hidden by the tablecloth. Antonio shot him an odd look. Bay flashed an innocent smile. He kept it in place, even as he draped one arm over Antonio's shoulders and reached beneath the table. Bay went straight for Antonio's crotch.

"What are you doing?"

"Exactly what it looks like." Bay kept his voice bland as he unzipped Antonio's pants and pulled out his cock. Antonio wasn't hard yet. He would be.

"Um. Are we about to go to jail?"

"Nope, but you are about to come in public. I thought you wanted me to try new things." Bay went to work. He didn't tease or play. Bay squeezed and tugged, working Antonio's dick with every intention of getting quick results. The waitress had only promised ten minutes. Otherwise, they weren't in anyone's line of sight. If Antonio was already uncomfortable anyway, he might as well get some joy from it.

Bay kissed Antonio's ear. His tongue dipped inside. Antonio released a pant and white-knuckled the edge of the table. "That's it," Bay whispered against his ear. He squeezed and shook Antonio's cock while teasing him with his words. "Come on, sexy. You don't want to get caught, do you? What if someone sees? Paint this carpet under the table with your cum. Fuck. I'm so hard, Nino. You have no idea how it murders me to stroke your dick and not be able to put it in my mouth or slip it inside my ass." A tiny whimper escaped Antonio. An evil smile tugged at Bay's lips. "Do it, Nino. If you come right now, I'll do any public act you ask of me, at any given time, no complaints. Come now." Antonio's hips lifted. His head fell back against Bay's shoulder. Bay felt Antonio's dick jerk. He immediately changed angles, shaking Antonio's cum out onto the floor. While Antonio still sucked air, Bay grabbed a napkin and cleaned up what he could.

When Antonio finally spoke, he sounded breathless. "You'll pay for that."

A chuckle that sounded evil, even to him, escaped Bay. "I don't doubt it, but it was totally worth it." He fixed Antonio's clothes before focusing on his food like nothing happened. It took Bay a second to realize Antonio seemed completely zoned out. His silence was quieter than normal. He looked Antonio's way again.

Antonio stared back with his heart in his eyes. For a moment, Bay wondered if Antonio was finally about to say the words. Instead, the moment passed, and Antonio stole a fry from Bay's plate. "Did you know the first French fries weren't actually made in France?"

Bay hid his disappointment by jumping into the conversation like nothing happened. "Really?"

"No. They were cooked in Greece."

A groan escaped Bay. "I take it my exposure therapy didn't work?"

Antonio's forehead crinkled as he held Bay's stare. "Exposure therapy?"

"You know, you're uncomfortable, so I make you extremely uncomfortable in hopes of alleviating the original discomfort."

A smile exploded across Antonio's face as the confusion cleared away. "I'm not uncomfortable. I just really like bad dad jokes."

A bark of laughter burst from Bay. He had never been so happy. "Don't go back to Vegas." The moment the words were out there, the guilt set in. He shook his head and looked away. That plea had been worse than confessing his love. Jesus. He was a mess. "Don't listen to me. You have your casino and a life in Vegas. That wasn't fair." He took a breath and met Antonio's stare again. Antonio looked intense again—the way he always did right before and after sex. The truth slipped from Bay. "I've never been this happy. Meeting you is the best thing that's ever happened to me. You're the best part of life."

"Do you need a to-go box for your food?"

Antonio tore his gaze away from Bay and focused on the waitress at her sudden appearance. "No. We prefer wrestling for our leftovers."

Bay burst into laughter. He was so in love with this ridiculous man. It would kill him when Antonio went back to Vegas, and the second thing Bay knew with absolutely certainty was that. Antonio would go back to his life in Vegas. Bay didn't stand a chance.

———

DON'T GO BACK TO VEGAS. THOSE WORDS KEPT playing over and over again in Antonio's head. He wanted to stay. Antonio just didn't know if he was strong enough to do what it took. With his legs thrown over Bay's lap, Antonio sent Derreck a text. He needed to check in to the casino while thinking about losing it.

Antonio: *Anything new or pressing?*

Derreck: *I'm good. Thanks for asking. Are you enjoying your trip?*

A smile tugged at Antonio's lips. Part of him missed seeing Derreck every day. They were friends. It was odd not having Derreck there, shadowing him and making sure he took his meds.

Antonio: *I'm good. Of course, I'm happy to hear you are as well.*

Derreck: *That's good to know. You are missed. Raiden stopped by this morning to drop off a wedding invitation. It seems he is marrying his Jason in two weeks. I meant to text you right after he left, but a million other things came up. He looks happy, though.*

Antonio: *That's great news. What is the day and time of the wedding?*

Derreck: *Two weeks from today, on a Monday of all days at noon. I don't recognize the address. I think it's a private residence.*

"You're smiling at your phone."

Antonio focused on Bay at the comment and shared the happy news. "My good friend Raiden is getting married. It seems an invitation was delivered this morning and the wedding is in two weeks. On a Monday at noon for whatever reason."

"That's awesome. I'm happy for your friend."

Antonio went back to staring at his phone. "I

should text him and let him know I'll be there. Hopefully, it won't be a huge affair and throw me into a panic attack. Should I ask him if I can bring a date?"

Bay massaged Antonio's thigh while staring absently at his own phone. Antonio didn't take it personally. He knew Bay needed to keep up to date with his patients. "Assuming this wedding is in Vegas, I'll likely have to pass. My vacation time is gone, but you have to go, for sure." A line appeared between his brows, as if something on his phone displeased him. Antonio wanted to ask, but he imagined, since it was patient-related, Bay wouldn't be able to share.

Damn. Antonio hadn't thought about Bay not being able to go back to Vegas with him, but it had been amazing having Bay all to himself for the past few weeks. He tossed his phone aside. Accepting Raiden's invitation could wait. He could take Derreck with him and avoid the fear of being alone. Right now, Bay looked unhappy and Antonio couldn't have that. He shifted positions and pushed Bay's phone aside before straddling Bay's lap.

"You're looking too serious over here. Have I left you unsatisfied too long after that amazing hand job in the restaurant? I cannot let my beautiful boy be unhappy."

Bay set his phone on the end table before wrapping his arms around Antonio. "I'm not unhappy. There's always a hum of desire around me when you're around. I don't need any extra incentive to be desperate for you. That hand job was hot, though. You looked sexy as hell while helpless against me."

Bay had no idea. Antonio was more than helpless against him. He was downright desperate. "I have a question." Antonio kissed Bay's chin, hoping to keep him somewhat distracted.

"Ask away." The breathless note to Bay's voice and the way he massaged Antonio's ass let Antonio know his ploy to keep Bay's attention split was working.

"Were you serious when you asked me to stay? Like, do you really want me here permanently?" Antonio worked on tearing open the front of Bay's pants to keep the conversation light.

Bay released a loud pant as Antonio shoved his hand inside Bay's underwear. "Yes. I want you here permanently. Why do you ask?"

"Just checking to see how hard I should be thinking about some things," he answered while slithering his way down Bay's body. He wouldn't make this talk a heavy one yet. Antonio needed to know Bay was completely serious about him first. That could wait another night. He licked Bay's dick, ensuring their talk came to an end. He was all about making Bay as happy as possible right now. Everything else could wait.

SEVEN

RAIDEN AND JASON'S WEDDING WAS AS beautiful as Antonio imagined it would be. It was small and intimate with less than twenty guests. It was—strangely—held in the back yard of a man's house who Antonio had banned from the casino... for punching Raiden. Life was funny sometimes. But the couple had looked at each other with so much love when they exchanged vows, Antonio had fought the urge to leave right then so he could get back to his heart. He had also learned the reason behind the Monday vows. It seemed Jason's brother hadn't been able to get a weekend flight and they had settled on a date that worked best for the only family the pair had left to be there.

Since Bay hadn't been free to come with Antonio

to Vegas due to the weekday, Antonio had wrangled Derreck into attending the wedding with him. That was another decision that had Antonio ready to rush out. By the time they made it back to the casino, Antonio had dodged all the sullen looks he could stand from Derreck. He knew the guy wasn't happy about how long Antonio had been gone. Antonio also knew that Derreck would be twice as aggravated when he heard Antonio's plans, but damn. Antonio needed to live for himself for once. They would always be friends, but Bay was in Phoenix. That was where Antonio wanted to be too. Plus, whether Derreck realized it or not, Antonio was holding him back too. Derreck needed to make a life for himself.

There were things to finalize here in Vegas, and then he could go back to Phoenix. He could confess his love and beg Bay to throw all good sense to the wind with him. After all, Raiden and Jason hadn't been together that long. No one had pointed that out like it was a bad thing. Love didn't wear a watch. Antonio's heart didn't understand waiting until other people wouldn't think he was nuts. He was in love with Bay. Caution was pointless now. He knew where he wanted to be, and it wasn't here.

"May I speak with you?"

Derreck's appearance in the doorway of

Antonio's office didn't surprise him. He had been waiting for Derreck to break all day, but Derreck's interruption did slow him down. That was irritating. He waved Derreck inside. "Of course." Antonio had never seen Derreck look so intense. He forgot his plans for a speedy exit at the sight of Derreck's dark expression. "Is everything okay?"

Derreck dropped his gaze to the floor and shuffled farther into the room. Antonio turned, following him. As he looked on, Derreck sat on the edge of Antonio's desk. His chest expanded as he took a deep breath before focusing on Antonio once more. He looked determined. "You've been gone a while."

Antonio pulled a face. "Yes. I know it leaves more responsibility on you. You deserve a raise for all you put up with from me. Which reminds me, I need to talk to you about the casino."

With a wave, Derreck brushed off Antonio's words, cutting off his confession. "This isn't about my workload or this place. The casino always runs smoothly. This is about you." Derreck held his stare. "You've really jumped in to being with this new guy with both feet. I barely heard from you while you were away."

Happiness swelled Antonio's chest. He needed

to talk about Bay. He wanted to tell Derreck everything. "I know it sounds crazy, since we haven't known each other that long. Truly, though, I think he is the one, Derreck. He makes me better. Forces me out of my shell while protecting me at the same time. I'm not sure anyone has ever looked at me the way he does. We're... equal." Antonio didn't know how else to describe them. While Antonio had been singing praises about his new relationship, Derreck had straightened away from the desk and moved closer. Antonio didn't notice until Derreck hovered over him, standing so close, Antonio was forced to tilt his chin up to keep holding Derreck's stare. Antonio's eyebrows snapped together. "Seriously, what's going on with you today? You've been more serious than necessary lately, but this is something else."

"I realized something important when you didn't come back right away."

"Okay." Antonio dragged out the word, confused as hell. "What?"

"Everyone has always wondered why I work so hard for you and why I'm always in your shadow, making sure you're taking your meds and getting enough rest. Obviously, it's because I care. We're friends. But with you gone, it hit me how much you mean to me." He took an audible breath. "I'm the one who's been looking out for you for years. Not this new guy. So I have to think you're as blind as I am. Otherwise, you'd know by now that I'm the one who loves you."

Before Antonio could let all that surprising news sink in, Derreck dropped his head. His mouth captured Antonio's. Antonio froze. His mind went blank before racing with a thousand questions. The biggest one of all was the most obvious. Why hadn't he seen this coming? Derreck had always been there, watching. Waiting. Antonio was such an idiot, and it was about to cost him his oldest friend, because he couldn't survive the alternative, losing Bay.

WHILE IT MIGHT HAVE TAKEN HIM CALLING IN some favors, all day of driving, and missing the actual wedding, Bay damn well made it to Vegas. He grabbed flowers from a cart outside the hotel before heading inside. A woman at the front counter pointed Bay in the direction of the offices where Antonio should be. He didn't stop to ask for permission before heading that way. No one tried stopping him. The second his feet crossed the threshold into Antonio's office, Bay's feet froze to the floor. Bay's heart stopped, and then it shattered. He had been so excited to get back to Antonio. All morning, he had been chuckling at the thought of Antonio's surprise. There was shock, all right. Too bad it was all Bay's. Tunnel vision had Bay incapable of looking away from Derreck and Antonio's kiss. His heartbeat sounded too loudly in his ears to know if he made a single sound.

Derreck's head lifted. He looked turned on and exactly like he stared down at the love of his life. Then, his head turned, and his gaze landed on Bay. For a second, they held each other's stare. Then, Bay turned away. His feet moved without thought, carrying him away from another heart break. Another cheating man. He was such an idiot. Always the fool. A young guy stood in his path, heading for the same scene Bay had just endured. Bay passed the flowers to him. Shock passed over the guy's features. If he said a word, Bay didn't hear. He needed to get back to Phoenix. Back to his job. That was all he had. Bay didn't know why he kept hoping for more.

"Excuse me. I'm sorry. Hold up a minute."

The fact that he was being chased finally penetrated Bay's blind attempt to escape. Bay turned the guy's way. He didn't see anything clearly, but he tried. The guy had sweet brown eyes. He looked innocent and Bay couldn't look away. "What do you want me to do with these flowers?" He squeezed the bouquet to his chest as he asked the question, as if no one ever gave him flowers.

Bay swallowed the hurt, but his voice still sounded like he had been chewing on glass when he spoke. "They're yours. I bought them for someone else, but—apparently—I was wrong."

A line appeared between the guy's brows. He looked adorably confused as his gaze swung toward Antonio's office and back Bay's way. His chest expanded and deflated as if someone punched him in the heart. His face cleared of all emotion. "I take it Derreck finally made his move on Nino and you must be Bay."

It was Bay's turn at the wheel of confusion. "How did you..."

"I'm Jett," Jett said, interrupting Bay. "I'm dating Derreck. Or, I was. I guess that's over." He dropped his gaze to the flowers and walked away.

Bay found himself going in pursuit. "You don't seem surprised."

Jett snorted and slowed enough for Bay to fall into step beside him. "Derreck has been in love with Nino for years. Anyone who looks close enough can see it, except Nino, of course. I guess I thought... I don't know what I thought." He flashed Bay a sad smile. "I'm sorry you were caught in the middle." He held the bouquet of roses a little closer to his chest. "Thank you for the flowers. Obviously, I know they weren't meant for me, and it's ridiculous for me to care, but no one ever gives me anything for no reason, so thanks."

"I..." Bay took a breath. He didn't know what he wanted to say. They had both gotten their hearts broken today. He felt moved to do something. Anything. "Would you like to go to dinner? I just drove in from Phoenix. I don't even know where I plan to stay now or anything at all, for that matter, but I know neither of us should be alone."

Jett flashed him a shy but grateful-looking smile. "Okay. I won't let you be alone."

Despite everything, a hint of humor crept in. Jett seemed so young and innocent. Bay was a caretaker to his bones. Maybe sticking with Jett was self-preservation, but Bay would take any life preserver he could get. Otherwise, he had nothing but time to face the reality of everything. He should have gone with his gut. Bay had known in his heart Antonio was too good to be true. He had been tricked in a well-played game by a master. Bay didn't think he could be blamed for falling for Antonio. That didn't change the outcome, though. He was still crushed. At least, with Jett at his side, he didn't have to hurt alone.

———————

THERE WASN'T ENOUGH ALCOHOL IN THE WORLD to soothe Antonio's heart. He had lost his oldest friend and Bay wasn't answering his calls. He couldn't get drunk enough to deal. No matter how he racked his brain, Antonio couldn't figure out how he had missed all the signs with Derreck. He hated that he had hurt his friend, but Antonio didn't feel the same. Maybe if Derreck had said something sooner or if Antonio hadn't met Bay. But things were different now. Antonio had made some decisions that were taking his life in a different direction. At least, he thought he had. Bay ignoring him had him fucked up. That on top of the Derreck thing had him lower than he had been in a long time. When he had come to Vegas this weekend, Antonio had been riding cloud nine. Obviously, there had been some trepidation about dropping some news on Derreck, but otherwise, nothing but sunshine and lollipops were on Antonio's radar for the foreseeable future.

Then it had all fallen apart. Now Antonio couldn't stop drinking the pain and fear away.

A shadow fell over Antonio's table before a body filled the empty seat at his table. Antonio's gaze fixed on the familiar figure. Jett's face was cold and hard. He looked nothing like the man Antonio used to date. Antonio finished off his drink before acknowledging Jett's presence. "How do you keep getting past security?"

Jett snorted. It was an ugly sound. "First off, you haven't been in town for a while. With Derreck in charge, things have changed. Secondly, with you selling out to Luna, you won't get to make the decision to bar me any longer. Third, fuck you and your feelings." Antonio blinked at Jett's words. This definitely wasn't the same man he had dated. The one who never talked back or broke character from being the needy boy. Jett wasn't finished. "You don't get to cheat on Bay with my man and then look down on me."

Everything inside Antonio went cold. Even with a thick layer of alcohol clouding everything, Jett had his attention. "What?"

Jett's cold sneer had Antonio's anxiety spiking. "You heard me. Poor Bay. You really crushed him. You should've seen his face after catching you kissing

Derreck. It was like finding his ex-husband in bed with another man all over again."

Antonio's fear had his temper snapping. "What in the fuck are you talking about?"

"You're such an idiot," Jett said, instead of answering. "Poor Derreck has been traipsing behind you, begging for you to notice him for years. Why do you think you can't keep anyone? Why do you think I ended up with someone else? Who do you think that someone else was? He's been sabotaging and undermining your every relationship forever now while just waiting to be noticed. You have no idea what it's like to love you, Nino. You're so cold and untouchable. Everything you do is calculated to get you whatever you want, but no one ever touches your heart. We're all just disposable bodies. Derreck couldn't resist me because you've touched me. Not for any other reason. Not because he wants me. Nobody ever really wants me," Jett tacked on, sounding absent. He focused on Antonio and his voice hardened again. "Maybe Bay will be next."

Without thought, Antonio's arm shot out, knocking the empty glasses from the table, sending them flying as his temper snapped. Every head turned their way as glass shattered in every direction.

Antonio didn't give a damn about any of that. "How the fuck do you know Bay?"

Jett calmly eyed the surrounding mess, as if his every day was like this one for him. His gaze finally moved back to focus on Antonio. "He was here earlier, flowers in hand, and ready to surprise you. It was very sweet. Until it wasn't. He said Derreck looked right at him. The two of you really know how to destroy people."

Antonio stood and took a step away. Even he didn't know where he was headed. Bay wouldn't answer his calls. His texts were ignored. He froze and turned Jett's way. "Wait. You've obviously been talking to Bay if you know about his ex. Where is he? Is he still in town? I have to fix things." Antonio didn't care if he sounded as desperate as he felt. Bay had seen Derreck kiss him. He thought the worst. Antonio had to make this right. Bay was out there somewhere hurting, and it was all Antonio's fault.

Jett dropped his gaze to his lap. He looked... damaged. For the first time, it truly hit Antonio. Everything Jett said was true. Before his stroke, Antonio had been a spoiled player. Afterward, he had become a withdrawn mess. Both versions of him were equally shitty. He did look for people's weaknesses so he could exploit them. Not once had he done so to cause harm, but his intentions didn't matter. He still ended up hurting people in the end. That wasn't Jett's fault.

"Derreck has only ever been a friend to me. I'm sorry I never noticed he had feelings for me and I'm sorry for my inability to be what you needed. Soon I'll be gone from here and you'll never have to think about me again. Neither will Derreck. You two can work things out or go your separate ways. Whatever you decide, you won't have to worry about me being a factor in that decision. I love Bay. I don't know what or how much he saw, but when Derreck kissed me, and I recovered from my shock, I immediately shut that down. He's always only been a friend in my eyes."

Jett visibly swallowed. He stood while keeping his gaze averted. "He's staying at the Luna tonight. Room fifteen-ten. He drove in to see you and plans to drive back tomorrow. I suppose he could change his mind and go home any time, though. He seemed pretty done with this place."

Despite the pains in his chest and his rapidly swelling throat, Antonio touched Jett's arm, bringing the man's gaze his way. "I'm really sorry, Jett. I feel terrible."

The hurt in Jett's eyes nearly buckled Antonio's

knees. Jett's gaze slid away again. "Fuck your feelings. No one ever really cares about anyone else."

Antonio's heart sank as Jett walked away. He genuinely hadn't meant to hurt anyone. Yet he had somehow hurt everyone. Some days, it felt like he couldn't win. When it came to Bay, Antonio had to try. There was no other option. He headed for the front door. Luna hotel wasn't that far. That was exactly why they wanted to acquire Antonio's casino. Lombardi was positioned on one corner of the street and Luna on the other. Luna planned to buy out the entire street and turn the area into an entire Luna experience. Nightclubs, restaurants, casino, wedding chapel, and an amphitheater where they could host bigger venues than the MMA fights they currently hosted. It was a massive undertaking. Antonio had been the only holdout before now. He hadn't wanted to give up his safe space before Bay. Now, it looked like he would lose both. That couldn't happen. Antonio would be isolated. Alone. His heart rate picked up and his vision narrowed. He tried to take stock of how much farther he had to go. Nothing looked familiar. Antonio tried taking a breath. It didn't help. He had to get to Bay.

Antonio dug out his phone. If he could just focus on something other than his surroundings, he could get to Bay. He called Bay's cellphone. When his call went to voicemail, Antonio started rambling. "I really wish you would answer your phone. I need to tell you so many things. Like, first off, it turns out Derreck has feelings for me, which I guess I should've known, but I didn't. Not until he kissed me. The second the shock wore off from my fucked-up stroke brain, I pushed him away." The phone beeped, ending the voicemail. Antonio quickly dialed again and started talking the second he was back in. "Fucking short voicemail time. Anyhow, I told him I didn't feel the same because I'm in love with you. He kind of shouted at me and stormed out. I tried texting and calling you right away, but you won't answer." The phone beeped again, cutting him off. With a growl, Antonio started the whole process over. This time, he didn't bother explaining he had been cut off. "I'm drunk, but I'm trying to get to you. Nothing looks familiar, though. Goddamn. I can't breathe." He stopped walking and looked around. Nothing felt real. No matter how hard he fought to breathe, it was like there was no air. He felt disconnected from the world. "I don't think I'm far. There's a big U with a park bench beneath. It seems like I recall that not being far from Luna. Goddamn. I really can't breathe. I need to sit down, but I swear

I'm trying to get to you." The beep cut him off again and Antonio headed for the bench. Logically, he knew a panic attack had him in its grip. Good sense didn't matter once terror set in. Antonio dropped on to the bench and bent at the waist. He fumbled with the phone and called Bay again. "My ex, Jett, says you're here. Please don't leave town until I can get to you."

"I didn't know Jett is your ex. He didn't tell me that part."

Antonio's head shot up as Bay's sexy voice gently washed over him. Bay was on his haunches in front of Antonio. When their gazes met, Antonio's vision blurred. Bay was really here. Jett hadn't been lying.

"Sit up, angel. Catch your breath." Bay took the phone from Antonio and stuffed it in his pocket before joining Antonio on the bench. "Lean this way," he said as he draped his arm over Antonio's shoulders and tucked Antonio against his side. Bay stroked Antonio's hair, soothing him. "Just relax."

The tension drained from Antonio. He snuggled close and took a few deep breaths. "I'm sorry. I was trying to get to you."

"I know." Bay's voice was so soothing that Antonio's mind cleared a bit. The way Bay kept stroking his hair had Antonio relaxing even more.

They sat together in silence. People walked by, but no one really looked their way.

Antonio fought a fresh wave of depression. He knew Bay showing up didn't mean Bay wasn't still done. Bay was a caretaker. That was all this was. "If you're done with me, will you ship Sparkle Feet back to me? Losing him and you might finally kill me."

Bay kissed his forehead. "I'm not done with you. Sparkle Feet isn't going anywhere. Right now, I'm hurt, beyond angry, and conflicted about how to deal with you living and working beside Derreck every day from now on, but I'm not done."

"I sold the casino."

Bay leaned away and met his stare. "What?"

Antonio nodded. "This afternoon, after the wedding, I sold the casino. The Kapra family—they own the Luna hotel and casinos—they've been after my place for a while. Before you, I never had a good enough reason to sell. It's my home and my safety net from becoming a full-blown hermit. Then I spent these last few weeks with you. When I was watching Raiden and Jason exchange their vows, I had an epiphany. You're the one for me. The only thing keeping me here is a building. So I called Zander Kapra this afternoon and accepted his latest offer."

Bay didn't look happy. In fact, his expression

didn't give away anything. "That building is a monument to a lifetime of hard work from you."

Antonio shrugged at Bay's claim. "What does that matter if I'm alone? Zander agreed to keep all the current staff in their current positions. So I'm free to..."

"Free to what?" Bay asked quietly, as if almost scared to know.

A smile touched Antonio's lips. He felt a bit stupid. Antonio had gotten caught up in the idea of being with Bay when there was a real possibility that Bay didn't feel the same. He straightened away, giving Bay some space. After bracing his hands on the edge of the bench, Antonio leaned forward and took a deep breath. His mind was finally clear enough to truly take in their surroundings. He really had almost made it to Bay's hotel. A bark of laughter escaped him. Antonio tried swallowing the sound. He shook his head as the feeling of being the world's biggest fool grew.

"I just met you a few weeks ago." He glanced over his shoulder.

Bay stared back at him, looking more intense than Antonio had ever seen him. "And?"

Antonio couldn't look away. It was crazy and ridiculous, but Antonio couldn't help the way he felt.

"And I'm completely in love with you. How is that possible? I've spent years trying to fall in love with everyone I meet, hoping for some purpose, but it never happened for me. Then you just show up one night at my hotel, and now here I am praying you'll love me back, because I've already given up everything to be with you."

Bay grunted out a laugh. A bitter-looking smile touched his lips.

Antonio had to know. "What?"

Bay's smile grew even as he shook his head. He released a loud sigh as his gaze locked on Antonio's, holding his stare. "I really thought you knew I'm hopelessly in love with you. For a while now, I honestly thought we were both fighting against being the one who said it first. All this time, you were completely blind to how I can't see a future without you anymore. You're such an adorable idiot."

In his drunken state, Antonio spent a moment trying to decide if he was supposed to be insulted or elated. "I don't... know how to respond to that."

Bay rolled his eyes and stood. He held his hand out for Antonio. "Let's go, baby. We need to grab my stuff from my room. If you're coming home with me permanently, we need to get you sober. We have to plan the best way to move your things to Phoenix."

As Antonio linked his fingers through Bay's, realization struck. Bay wasn't done with him. They weren't over. Antonio's throat swelled. He couldn't look away from Bay. "I really love you."

A sweet smile touched Bay's lips. "I really love you too."

Hand in hand, they made their way inside the Luna hotel. Antonio was still drunk, and his mind wasn't completely clear, but he understood the highlights. Bay loved him. He wasn't alone in a dark hell of anxiety any longer. Most importantly, Antonio realized they wouldn't be easily broken. When Antonio finally sobered up, he would make sure Bay knew his worth. He would never let Bay doubt him again.

ON THE OUTSIDE, BAY WAS CALM AND collected. On the inside, Bay was enraged and shaking with fear. He wanted to find Derreck. Bay wanted to be someone he wasn't. He wanted to destroy the man who had tried to ruin his relationship with the only person to love him for real. The fear came from someplace deeper. He couldn't describe the anguish of thinking he had lost Antonio the same way he had lost Matty. It was insane. Matty had been his husband and Bay had caught him literally having sex with someone else. Yet, seeing another man kissing Antonio—a guy Bay had only being seeing a few weeks—had been a thousand times worse than losing Matty. That scared him shitless. If the day came—after years together — that Bay truly lost Antonio the way he had Matty, Bay might not survive it. Also, that goddamned panic attack. Bay had never seen one that bad. If Bay hadn't rushed out to get Antonio, or Antonio hadn't called, Bay couldn't breathe at the thought of what might have happened to him. Would he have continued spiraling until he gave himself a heart attack? Maybe someone would have used the opportunity to harm him. Goddamn, he could not let anything happen to Antonio. Bay loved him more than he loved himself.

It wasn't helping Bay's nerves that Antonio still looked like he might cry at any moment.

While Bay repacked his bag and checked out of his hotel, Antonio stood off to the side. He never made a sound. In fact, Bay didn't think Antonio as much as turned his head to take in his surroundings. Bay thought he might be checked out from reality until Antonio pulled out his wallet and swiped a key card on the elevator at Lombardi so the elevator would go to the penthouse. When the doors opened and they stepped out, Bay turned in a circle and checked out the place Antonio had been living in for years. Bay had expected an expensive-looking hotel room. He was wrong. It was literally an entire floor of the hotel. The elevator opened into a huge open space. Windows surrounded them, showing the Vegas skyline. Bay was awed. He thought he understood what Antonio planned to give up for him until he stood inside Antonio's private space. This place was amazing. It was so much more than the life Bay offered in Phoenix. His throat swelled.

"If I had seen this the weekend we met, I'm not sure I would have let you pursue me."

Antonio glanced Bay's way as he emptied his pockets onto a nearby table. "I love how you said that —like I would've given you a choice in the matter." Despite the cold confidence behind Antonio's words, he still sounded like he had been chewing on glass.

Bay couldn't let the topic go. Antonio's life was so much bigger than Bay's. "I'm being serious. How can you think about giving this up for me? I'm nothing compared to this place you've built."

When Antonio's gaze met Bay's again, Bay's breath caught at Antonio's intensity. He was almost frightened in that moment. "You're talking about two things that have no comparison. This is a place." Antonio looked around. "Truthfully, it has been almost a prison for the past few years." The blue eyes that made Bay's heart beat a little faster pinned him in place again. "You are a living, breathing person. The man who set me free. The man I love." A smile lit Antonio's face, making it a little easier for Bay to breathe. "Plus, the Kapra family is paying me two billion dollars for this place. Billion with a B. I have ten million invested in it. That's an offer I can't refuse."

For a moment, Bay's brain refused to work. Most people couldn't truly fathom how much a billion dollars was. It was more than could be spent in a lifetime. Not only was Antonio talking about two billion, he said it as if people threw that much money around every day. Before he could form words, the elevator doors opened behind him, forcing his attention on their uninvited guest.

Derreck stepped out. His amber gaze moved between them. There was zero emotion in his expression. With his hands clasped behind his back, he looked like he held back a river of feelings he didn't want to show.

Antonio growled.

Bay's stomach muscles automatically tightened. Antonio made that same sound when he fucked Bay. It was hot. Now wasn't the time. His body didn't care.

"Today isn't the day to test boundaries with me by using your security clearance card to come to my place unannounced."

Derreck gave Antonio a sharp nod. "I'm aware, but I knew you wouldn't talk to me if I asked." His gaze shifted Bay's way. "And I need to say I'm sorry."

Bay moved to a leather couch near the window. "This is all you, baby," he said as he passed Antonio. There was no point in him getting involved. He had already won. Antonio belonged to him. This was something Antonio needed to handle.

Antonio brushed fingers with Bay before squaring off against Derreck. "Only because we've been friends for years, you have two minutes."

"Understood." Derreck moved farther into the room. His chest expanded as he took a breath. "I'm sorry. For years, I've been looking after you and you know I don't really have anyone else I call family. I panicked. Kapra has been after this place for years. You and this casino are all that I have. When you left for Phoenix and stayed gone for so long, I knew you'd sell and leave me behind."

Antonio cleared his throat. It sounded painful. "I wasn't aware you knew about Kapra, but I guess that explains how Jett knew."

A deep line appeared between Derreck's eyebrows. "When did you talk to Jett?"

Antonio ignored Derreck's question. "If you'd bothered to talk to me, instead of assuming the worst of me, I would've explained that I had already worked out a deal for you with Zander. When he takes control of the hotel, he has to keep you in your current position, making at least your current pay, or offer you a severance of a minimum of two hundred thousand dollars. He seemed happy to keep you where you are. It's in his best interest to keep things running smoothly, and you do that. As to being left behind, I always believed we would be friends no matter where I live. I guess I was wrong."

The line between Derreck's eyebrows deepened. "Did it occur to you that I might not want to work for the mafia?" Bay's eyebrows shot to his hairline at that comment, but he didn't interrupt. "And, seriously, when did you talk to Jett? He's out of town. Did he call you? Are you two still talking?"

Bay couldn't hold back any longer. He was tired of being quiet. "Actually, Jett came back early. It seems he's the same as me. He planned to surprise you and ended up being the one surprised. He was standing behind me when you kissed Antonio."

Derreck scrubbed his hands over his face before turning his chin up to stare at the ceiling. When he focused on Bay again, he looked wrecked. "What did he say?" His voice sounded worse than his expression.

Antonio answered before Bay could. "That you're the one he cheated on me with and you've been wrecking my relationships for years."

Derreck spun away and made an angry gesture before turning back Antonio's way. "That's not true. Not all of it."

"It doesn't matter." Antonio's words sounded every bit as done as Antonio looked. "If you can't talk to me, your oldest friend in the world, then why are you here now? What are you trying to salvage? We must not have the friendship I thought we did if you just couldn't talk to me."

"You're right."

To Bay's surprise, Derreck left without further argument—like they really were done for good.

Antonio stared at the closed elevator doors for much longer than necessary after Derreck was gone. Bay swore he could feel the hurt rolling off Antonio in waves. Despite everything, Derreck had been

Antonio's friend forever. Derreck was the one who had taken care of Antonio after his stroke. That wasn't the kind of friendship that a person easily lost.

Bay stood and closed the distance between them. He drew Antonio back against his chest, wrapping him in his embrace. Bay skimmed his lips across the shell of Antonio's ear. "Do you want me to chase him down and strap him to a chair so you can torture the truth from him?"

He felt Antonio's muscles relax. Antonio melted against his chest. "No. I already know the truth. He's scared of being abandoned. I can't fix that. I truly feel as if I'm failing everyone, though. It says a lot about me that no one feels like they can talk to me."

Bay couldn't stop touching Antonio everywhere he could reach. Damn. Holding Antonio was like embracing heaven. His heart felt light and heavy at the same time. He needed more. His lips found the side of Antonio's neck. "You're so damn beautiful inside and out. That scares people." Bay spoke between kisses. He couldn't stop brushing his lips against Antonio's skin. Bay had almost lost this. That couldn't happen. "Most people, when they look like you, they're ugly on the inside. Everyone knows how to deal with that—take it or leave it. You put people out of balance, because it's like you don't know you're beautiful."

Antonio snorted as he turned in Bay's arms. He snuggled against Bay's chest, letting Bay hold him. "I can't care about anyone else right now. Everything still hurts from almost losing you. It terrifies me that you might still change your mind. You could go back to Phoenix and forget about me. That kills me."

Bay's arms tightened around Antonio. "That's not true in the least. Losing you would kill me. I've been sitting in my hotel room all day, trying to make myself leave this town. Without you, there's nothing for me to go home to." Bay sucked in a breath. It sounded ragged even to his ears. "Honestly, I'm petrified by how far I would go and how much I would forgive just so I wouldn't lose you." Antonio had no idea how much Bay meant his claim. His eyes stung at the thought of Antonio cheating on him, and Bay couldn't say he wouldn't forgive that. Bay was boring. It was always only a matter of time before people noticed. He felt sick. Bay had never loved someone this much.

Antonio's chin lifted. His eyes looked fierce as he focused on Bay. "You are mine. No one hurts you. Not even me." Antonio pulled Bay down for a kiss. The gentle Italian he had fallen in love with was gone. Bay had obviously angered him, so Bay accepted his punishment. "I love you," Antonio growled against his lips as he tore at Bay's clothes. Bay dutifully lifted his arms and let Antonio have his shirt when he leaned away. "You don't get to accept whatever bullshit gets thrown your way. You are to be respected."

Bay lost his breath. "Goddamn. You're always hot, but your rage is sexy as hell."

Antonio's eyes flashed fire as they focused on Bay. "Matty's loss was my gain, but no one breaks your heart. That's my heart. I could never do you harm, but if you think I am hurting you, you had damned well better not stand by and take it. You are worth more than everyone else. I expect you to know it. Now finish getting undressed and get in my bed."

Lust choked Bay. No one understood what it was like to be loved by Antonio. When he turned dark and possessive, it rendered Bay useless. All he could do was obey. He peeled off his clothes with his gaze locked on Antonio's every move. Antonio angrily wrenched off his clothes and tossed them aside—like they offended him. Bay expected him to punch a hole in the wall any second. Part of Bay wanted to psychoanalyze why that had him so hard that pre-cum already ran down his length. The rest of Bay cared not at all why he found Antonio's anger so arousing. He just really wanted Antonio to fuck him with all the rage flashing in his eyes.

While Bay waited on the bed, Antonio tore open the bedside drawer with so much force, he yanked the drawer out into the floor. He bent and scooped out a bottle of lube. His gaze fixated on Bay. The flush on his cheeks might have been lust or anger. Probably both. Either way, Bay was ready. He practically panted through watching Antonio coat his cock with lube. Without thought, Bay palmed his erection and stroked. He needed relief. With no warning, Antonio snagged Bay's ankle and dragged him to the edge of the bed. A whimper escaped Bay. He tried biting back the sound. Antonio pushed Bay's knees up and impaled him. Bay cried out. He nearly came again in one thrust the way he had their first time together.

Antonio's gaze met his. "Play with yourself. I want to watch."

Bay didn't need to be told twice. He immediately stroked himself, biting back cries as Antonio rocked forward. Antonio hit at the perfect angle. Bay squeezed his eyes shut. Stars flashed behind his closed lids. The sound of skin slapping skin filled the air as Antonio fucked him with no mercy. Bay tugged at his cock, reaching for the release that was just out of reach. Antonio felt so good inside him. Too good.

"Look at me, Bay."

Bay's eyes shot open. Antonio's intense stare waited for him. The moment Antonio had Bay's attention, he tweaked Bay's balls in just the right way, sending Bay into oblivion. He open mouth gasped for air as a spasm nearly jack-knifed him from the bed. Hot cum hit his bottom lip. Antonio's harsh expression never softened.

"Lick your lip clean, Bay. I want to watch."

Bay took his time. He slowly swiped his tongue across his bottom lip while holding Antonio's stare. Salt tickled his taste buds. A loud pant burst from Antonio. His entire body stiffened as if watching Bay sent him over the edge. Everything became clearer in that moment than ever before. Bay finally understood why he felt closer to Antonio than anyone else he had ever met. He hadn't fallen in love too fast. Bay had met his other half and his soul had recognized Antonio immediately. Their souls had simply been waiting for their hearts and brains to catch up. There had never been any chance they could hurt each other, because there had never been any chance they could live without each other. It was fate. Bay wouldn't doubt them again.

EIGHT

AFTER A FULL NIGHT OF SLEEP IN BAY'S ARMS, waking up sober and with the man he loved, Antonio finally felt halfway human again. In some ways, it hadn't fully hit him yet that his life was about to change. Soon, he would no longer call Vegas home. His gaze moved Bay's way. A drop of water fell from Bay's hair and ran down his bare back. Even after having Bay in the shower, Antonio wasn't satisfied. He wondered how many years it would take to ease the hunger. A smile tugged at his lips. He would find out.

Antonio leaned close to the mirror and tried shaving. He growled in frustration. It had been ten goddamn years and still he struggled with everyday shit. He hated this bullshit so much. He caught Bay staring. Bay looked sexy as hell with his skin still moist from the shower and steam lingering in the air. He looked way too sexy to be with someone as fucked up as Antonio.

Antonio pulled a face. "Goddamn intention tremor. Sometimes, it makes it impossible to do anything."

Bay didn't bat an eyelash. He closed the distance between them. "Here, baby. Let me." He took the razor from Antonio. Antonio stood still. While Bay kept his gaze locked on his task, Antonio stared at Bay. Bay looked steady and capable. He didn't look anything like the shy and awkward man Antonio met that first weekend in Vegas. Right now, Bay was the confident doctor. Antonio waited until Bay leaned away to rinse the razor to say what weighed on his mind the most.

"This is hard for me. I'm used to being the caretaker. That's my role."

Bay's dark blue gaze locked on to Antonio and didn't budge. "We take turns taking care of each other. You make sure I eat and sleep. I step in when you need help." His eyes sparkled with laughter. "Welcome to being in a healthy give and take relationship. Do you think you can handle it?"

Antonio thought about the way Bay had swept in

at the restaurant that one night and stepped outside his comfort zone, stopping a panic attack before it took hold. He turned every moment of them over in his head while Bay finish shaving him. Antonio didn't find his answer until Bay helped wiped away the final bits of shaving cream.

"I think I can handle almost anything as long as we're in it together. Meeting you is the best thing that's happened to me in a long time. I know you worry, because your ex was complete shit, but I could never hurt you."

A small smile passed over Bay's features. "I know. That doesn't mean I'm not still completely enraged with Derreck."

"As you should be," Antonio said, because Derreck had seen Bay standing there and chosen to hurt him. Even though Derreck had been his friend for years, Antonio wasn't sure he could forgive that. He wasn't sure he would ever forgive himself either. Antonio felt pretty insecure about a lot of things at the moment. He had to make it stop before the anxiety took hold again. Antonio decided to try Bay's way of staving off panic. He jumped in with both feet. "Do you remember when you swore to me that you would perform one public act with me, no questions or arguments?"

A smile exploded across Bay's face. No doubt, he expected anything. "I recall promising something to that effect, yes."

"Will you honor it?"

"Of course," Bay said, as if slightly offended Antonio would think otherwise.

Antonio was about to test that. "Good. I'm calling that in. Marry me."

Bay's expression snapped closed, stealing Antonio's chance to get read on his thoughts. "I'm sorry. What?"

"Marry me," Antonio repeated. "Let's get dressed, go next door to the Luna wedding chapel, and get married. I need you to know that you're it for me. Forever. I don't want anyone else."

"You don't have to marry me to prove—"

"You swore one public act of my choosing without argument. I hear arguing."

Bay blinked. He moved away and started dressing. "Okay. Let's go."

It was Antonio's turn to freeze. "Are you sure? Just like that?"

A laughing gaze shot his way. "Shush, Nino. Get dressed so we can go."

Antonio didn't budge. "I don't want you to resent

being married to me because you didn't want it. I withdraw my request."

In a flash, Antonio found himself crowded against the counter with an irate Bay hovering over him. "Stop it, Nino. I love you. You gave up your life here in Vegas for me. I have no qualms about giving up my name. People will probably think we're crazy. Hell, maybe we are. But do you know what? I don't give a fuck," Bay said, not waiting for Antonio to answer. "Matty and I were together for years before we got married. It made no difference at all. He still wasn't faithful to me, and you know what else? I wasn't surprised. You're different. When I look at you, I know I matter. Maybe one day you will get sick of me, but I know you'll say it and let me fight for you. I also believe with all my heart you'll fight for me too. Are you scared of that life? I'm not."

Damned if Bay didn't sum up all Antonio's thoughts, as if he read his mind. "No. I'm not afraid. This is the life I want."

Bay kissed him. Hard. "Get dressed, sexy. We have a life to start."

With his heart in his throat and his eyes stinging from the happiness, Antonio did as told. He wanted the life Bay painted. There was no time like the present to grab ahold of everything his heart needed. Everything he heart desired was Bay.

———

I<small>T TURNED OUT THEY HAD TO WAIT A FEW HOURS</small>. All of Bay's important papers were back in Phoenix. While Antonio had hired a private service to fly to Phoenix and pick up what Bay needed, they still had to wait. Even with hours to think, Bay didn't change his mind. It wasn't until the paperwork was out of the way that Bay's mind slowed at all. As he held Antonio's hands and listened to the man officiating the ceremony, Bay rejoined reality. A smile tugged at his lips. He wasn't scared at all. As he had once told Antonio, Bay didn't believe in regrets. Every decision he had ever made in his life had led him here. Bay couldn't wait to spend his life with Antonio.

"If anyone has any reason why these two shouldn't marry, speak now or forever hold your peace."

Antonio's smile grew to match Bay's. There was no one there but them and some lady who worked for the chapel as an official witness.

"Wait. Wait. You're not getting married without me." Bay's forehead furrowed as his gaze shot to the chapel entrance. An extremely tall and beautiful man with gorgeous tan skin and of obvious Asian descent rushed down the aisle. Derreck followed at a slower pace. When they settled in next to the official witness, the beautiful guy in a light blue dress motioned impatiently. "Okay. Continue."

Bay met Antonio's gaze. Antonio wore a huge smile. Bay decided he could ask questions later. The wedding got under way and passed in a blur of happiness and surreality. When it came time to exchange rings, Bay almost groaned until their new arrival passed a tiny box Antonio's way.

Antonio pulled out a gorgeous ring with three diamonds. "Raiden is very good at handling things, but if this doesn't fit or if you don't like it, we'll deal with that later."

Bay's face hurt from smiling while Antonio slipped the ring on his finger. It was a little loose, but it worked. Antonio plucked a second ring from the box and handed it to Bay so Bay could do his part. The simple gold band easily slid onto Antonio's finger. Seconds passed and they were declared partners for life. Antonio overcame him. He heard a wolf whistle pierce the air as Antonio claimed his mouth. There was so much happiness vibrating from Bay, he wondered if he glowed. He was in love. It was beautiful and made all the heartache and waiting worthwhile. Bay's life was complete.

The moment their kiss ended; Bay found himself engulfed in a hug. "I'm Raiden," Raiden said as he squeezed Bay. He smelled good. Bay also thought he might break the guy if he hugged him back too hard.

"It's nice to meet you, Raiden. I'm sorry I didn't make it in time to be at your wedding."

Raiden waved off his words. "Don't worry over it at all. Truthfully, I don't think I noticed who was there. I was too happy."

As Raiden moved on to exclaim over Antonio, Bay's gaze moved Derreck's way. He hung back a bit, looking more than a little unsure of his welcome. Bay tried for a smile. He was pretty good at being the bigger man. There was no reason why he couldn't be that person again today. After all, Antonio had married him. Derreck couldn't break that.

"Thanks for coming," Bay said, holding his hand out for Derreck to shake. "I think, once the excitement wore off, Nino would've been heartbroken if you hadn't been here."

Derreck accepted his handshake. He looked like hell, but he still smiled. "Congrats, man. I can see that he loves you. All I've ever wanted was for him to be happy. He's probably not feeling it right now, but we're family. I couldn't miss his big day."

Antonio slipped his fingers through Bay's, pulling Bay's attention his way. Antonio's gaze was locked on Derreck. "Thank you for bringing Raiden and picking up the rings. I don't know what I would've done without you."

While looking sheepish, Derreck shrugged. "You're my best friend. Just because I never like for things to change doesn't mean I don't want you to have the best life you can. I'm sorry I didn't say that yesterday rather than freaking out at the thought of being alone in the world again." While they continued making small talk, Bay eyed the pair. He didn't know what would happen between them once Bay had Antonio settled in Phoenix. Strangely, he hoped they remained friends. It had never been Bay's intention to steal anything from Antonio. Hell, only a few weeks ago, he fully expected Antonio to be the one who took everything. Bay's gaze slid Antonio's way. In a way, Bay had been right. Antonio had stolen everything from him. His loneliness, his fears, and his heart. In fact, Bay couldn't wait to see what Antonio took from him next. He hoped it was his clothes. A smile tugged at the corners of Bay's mouth at the thought. This man was his home. Being inside him every night for the rest of his life sounded like the happiest future possible.

Keep an eye out for the next Messy Hearts, *Love-Blocked*.

Please consider clicking this link and leaving a review, https://www.amazon.com/review/create-review?asin=B082FQYHLG. Reviews really help with a book's visibility, which ensures I can continue writing. Thank you, Charity.

ABOUT THE AUTHOR

Charity Parkerson is an award winning and multi-published author with several companies. Born with no filter from her brain to her mouth, she decided to take this odd quirk and insert it in her characters.

*Eight-time Readers' Favorite Award Winner
  *2015 Passionate Plume Award Finalist
  *2013 Reviewers' Choice Award Winner
  *2012 ARRA Finalist for Favorite Paranormal Romance
  *Five-time winner of The Mistress of the Darkpath

Connect with her online:

—Sign up for my newsletter: http://bit.ly/CharityNews
  —Join my readers' group on Facebook: http://bit.ly/CharitysTribe
  —Website: charityparkerson.com

—Facebook:
facebook.com/authorCharityParkerson
facebook.com/TheMenofSin
—Twitter: twitter.com/CharityParkerso
—Instagram: Instagram.com/sinnerauthor

www.ingramcontent.com/pod-product-compliance
Lightning Source LLC
Chambersburg PA
CBHW061243170626

46809CB00007B/2799